What is being said about *Messing with God's Country*:

"Seasoned planned giving professional and author Melissa Laird has crafted a tale to remind us that danger can arise in even the most sedate of professions. *Messing with God's Country* demonstrates that environmentalists are not only people who climb trees and blockade bulldozers. More often they are fundraisers and planned giving officers who knock on doors never knowing exactly what they'll find on the other side."

~Dan Asher, President, Foundation Management Group, LLC, Seattle, Wa.

"Enchanted by the Pacific Northwest, we are proud to recommend *Messing with God's Country*, a compelling sojourn into the sights and sounds of Seattle at the turn of the millennium. The reader is treated to fascinating characters who bring to life causes and concerns we still confront today."

~Gov. James and Jessica Doyle, Madison, Wisconsin

"*Messing with God's Country* is a boldly different type of read. This vivid book by Melissa Laird is a combination novel and amended regional memoir: a book you make connections with through scents and sounds of the city of Seattle. There is jazz royalty, people and places of pride that at one moment suggest a sentimental journey and the next a formidable crime novel."

~Nashira Priester, Northwest writer and poet.

"This book is propelled by sensitive descriptions and observations of Seattle and the Pacific Northwest and a writer who cares about preserving the area. Additionally, the book builds to a page-turning thriller at the end."

~ Jean Walkinshaw, Emmy-award winning filmmaker and PBS producer

Messing with God's Country includes in its backdrop the vibrant Seattle jazz scene of the late 90s. The characters move with the spirit of the art form. Garret, in the midst of change, uncertainty, and challenge, is fueled by the music as he begins to tune in to his true self, to do the right thing, and to discover the ultimate beauty of nature.

~ Maggie and Todd Zimberg, Island Jazz Quintet

Messing With God's Country

†

BY

Melissa Laird

Some names and identifying details have been changed to protect the privacy of individuals.

Book and Cover design: Vladimir Verano, Third Place Press

Cover Photo © Keith Lazelle of Quilcene, Washington.
www.keithlazelle.com

Lyrics by Jon Hendricks to the tune "Moanin'"
by Bobby Timmons, used with permission.

Edited by Jessica Levey

ISBN: 978-0-615-91950-8

Printed at Third Place Press, Lake Forest Park,
on the Espresso Book Machine v.2.2.
thirdplacepress.blogspot.com
www.thirdplacepress.com

Acknowledgements

Thanks to my parents Pat and Dick Laird who said they wanted to write a novel.

Thank you to those who have read drafts and egged me on over the years: Gloria Newman, Barry Malzberg, the late Lois Phillips Hudson, teacher extraordinaire, and Linda Kozarek. And to those who helped wave me in during the final rounds: Leslie Brown, Deb Crespin, Jessica Doyle, Christina Harrison, Fayette Krause, Maggie Laird, Nashira Priester, Shelley Rolfe and Cinthia Smith.

Thanks to my Overall clan: Charles and our sons Carlos and Kassa.

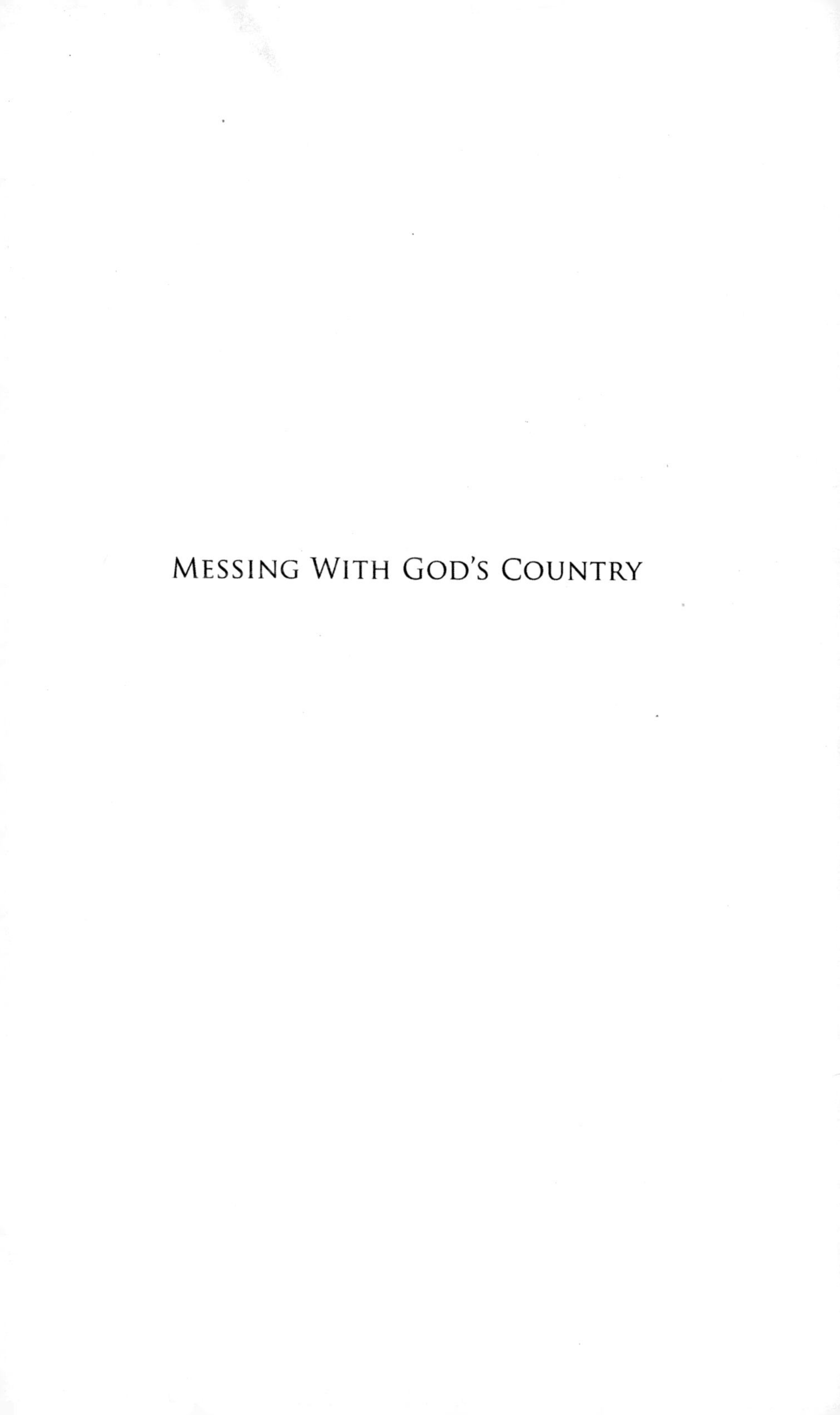

Messing With God's Country

Chapter One

†

Spring, 1999

"See Garret, I've got this property up on the Skagit River and I want the conservation folks to get it—Ruthie's group. They know what's going on up there, bringing back the eagles and all."

Arnie was sitting in a rocking chair with a blanket over his legs. His face was pale, thin, and translucent. "Some people don't know this, but the Skagit is the place where most of the King salmon of Puget Sound go to spawn."

Ruthie nodded. Arnie began to rock slowly as he spoke. "A few years ago, I went up on one of those Skagit boat trips in the winter when all the eagles were down from Alaska. We counted 260 eagles along ten miles of river. In one section, we saw about sixty eagles all perched in two trees as if they had been revived from the dead." Arnie began to cough dryly. "I wish I could have done more—like volunteer up there." He turned and coughed to the side. "It just—it didn't work out like I thought."

"Don't you feel bad now, Arnie," Ruthie told him. "What you're doing for the river, well, it's fabulous. You're donating an enormously important piece of waterfront property—saving it for all the wildlife and the people who depend on it."

Arnie's wife Rhea brought him a glass. "Arnie, here's some water. It's not too cold." She held the glass as he sipped through a straw. Turning toward Ruthie she said, "He gets it down better that way. That chemotherapy—it messes up your tastebuds.

What can I get for you two? Cranberry juice? Or how about some nice hot tea?"

"Oh I'm fine, Rhea. Garret?" Ruthie looked over at him and he shook his head. "Rhea, why don't you just take a load off?"

Rhea sat down on a stool next to her husband.

"See Garret, it's the whole watershed up there that's important," Arnie continued. "You say you're new to Seattle?"

"Brand new. I'm from Chicago." He felt like adding that the move to Seattle had been too abrupt, that his mind hadn't caught up yet. But the job wasn't supposed to be about his feelings. It was about the client's.

"Well, if you cut down too many trees, then soil washes into the river and gets trapped in the gills of the salmon and buries their eggs. But the eagle's become the symbol for the watershed. Living on salmon carcasses, the eagle's the litmus test. Heck, there's nothing more American. I figure if you can't even protect the symbol of America, you oughta pack up and go back to Europe." He began to cough again, and Rhea patted him on the back.

"He gets so worked up," she said.

"Well, I wish more people had the awareness he has," Ruthie told her.

"He has good days and bad days. You know Garret, he was in remission for several months, and then *poof!* Just like that—the cancer flared up again."

Arnie sighed with what Garret thought was almost irritated resignation and said, "That's why I need to get this taken care of." He reached under a newspaper and pulled out a large manila envelope. "Ruthie, these are the keys to the property and the deeds. You go on up and have a look," he said, pulling the group of keys out to show her. "And Garret, if you're going to be the banker, then you go on up, too. This first silver key is for the garage, and this one's to the well—it's got little Chinese characters on it. And that brass key gets you into the cabin. It's way back behind the garage through the woods. My son-in-law Dan still has the key to the gate, but you can go around it on foot." Arnie handed over the envelope and began to rock slowly.

"Does your daughter feel okay about this donation?" Garret asked him. As a trust officer, he wasn't about to get mixed up in any family squabbles. Arnie didn't seem to hear him.

"I think Dede's comfortable with whatever her father wants to do," Rhea answered instead.

Through the doorway into the family room, Garret could see Puget Sound and a section of beach called Golden Gardens.

Arnie cleared his throat. "Put it this way. It's our property and it's up to us to decide what happens to it. Dede and her husband Dan and my son—they're doing pretty well. I just want to make sure that Rhea gets something out of this. This annuity deal she's getting from the bank is just like a pension. It makes more sense than owning land she never gets to see. She doesn't even drive. My idea has always been this land should be protected from development."

"Well, Mr. McGowan, I don't want to rush anything, but it seems to me that as soon as we look over the property, we ought to get you some paperwork to transfer it to the conservation group."

"Fine by me. You can let my son-in-law Dan take a quick look at the papers. He's a lawyer, you know. Kind of looks after family affairs."

"Of course," Garret said. "Does he have a copy of your will by any chance?"

"Yup, he's got it. I'll tell him to send that over to you along with those papers." Arnie stopped rocking. "You know, we always thought that land would be a nice place to take the family. Once we got the cabin built, one thing led to another and I got sick. We never really had enough time..." His voice faded and he began wheezing.

Rhea patted his back again softly. "Arnie, you're going to need a nap." Glancing at Ruthie and Garret she said, "He gets very tired out, you know. I'm not trying to rush you folks." Turning back to her husband, she got up from the stool. "You want to take it here on the sofa, dear? I can put on one of your CDs. Which one do you want to hear?"

"Better make it the Ellington."

Garret noticed the stack of CDs—mostly Ellington, Count Basie and other big band stuff. Arnie got on the couch and Rhea opened the CD player.

"Arnie's one of those people who thinks about jazz like it's food."

"Sounds like my dad," Garret noted.

"What about you, son?" Arnie asked, resting his head against a pillow.

"I used to play tenor sax in high school and college—even got a few soloist awards, actually."

"And then you just quit?"

"Pretty much. I guess I ran out of steam and thought I needed a real job." For Garret, giving up playing his horn was something like pretending the Eastern hemisphere didn't exist.

Arnie nodded as if he understood. "In this country, real jazz musicians have a rough go of it. Just the same, if I had that kind of talent I'd be blowing the thing every chance I got." Duke started bubbling out "In a Mellow Tone," his silky big band sound taking over the room like concentric circles of water.

"So who's your favorite sax player?" Arnie pressed.

"That would have to be Coltrane."

"Oh right. John Coltrane. I should have some of him around here myself. Rhea, he's the one who was playing "My Favorite Things" on the radio the other day, remember? She likes the Broadway stuff, but she could tell he was good," he said in a confiding tone.

He adjusted his pillow and his eyes closed as if a magnet had pulled them shut. "You hold onto those keys now, Ruthie. And stick with this guy Garret. He's solid but he's versatile."

Ruthie winked at Garret.

Rhea lowered the volume on the CD player. "As I said, he has good days and bad days. Food just doesn't taste any good to him. I'm constantly trying to find something that he can get down."

"Rhea, how about something from Pike Market? I could pick up some local fish and some fresh vegetables?" Ruthie suggested.

"Oh, thank you, dear. Dede has been doing that, but thank you for the offer." She spread the blanket over Arnie's shoulders and walked them to the door.

On Market Street, when somebody swerved into her lane suddenly Ruthie had to jam on her brakes, but she seemed unfazed. "Thanks for asking Arnie about how his children feel," she said, glancing over at him.

"That's just part of my job," Garret said.

"I had no clue how Rhea felt, because every time I called she put Arnie right on the phone."

"So they come to Seattle for the cancer treatments?"

"Yeah. They drive down from Bellingham, and usually stay for at least a week. The house belongs to their daughter and son-in-law. But Arnie's beginning to look a little weary to be making that drive."

Garret nodded, wishing he could think of something reassuring to say about the cancer treatments. "What did Arnie do for a living?"

"He worked for the Department of Agriculture for many years—very high up in that bureaucracy."

"An intriguing guy, for sure. He's smart, seems like the real deal," he added. As they drove up to the steel grating of the Ballard Bridge, he noticed Ruthie had a leotard on under her blouse.

He hadn't met many botanists before, especially not lovely female ones. He wanted to ask her about her work, but he didn't want to say anything corny. As she glanced in his direction, her eyes sparkled like cool water, yet there was a warmth to them. Did growing up in the Northwest make someone seem closer to nature? He had no clue how to phrase a question like that.

She turned on the radio of the company car. "People are always changing these pre-sets."

She wore no rings, but did that mean she was single? He had questions, but he was on the job and wasn't going to be pushy. And after all, he had promised himself he would keep business separate from pleasure. He'd seen enough people shoot themselves in the foot by mixing the two at his old job.

They rode the rest of the way making friendly small talk, and when Ruthie dropped him at his office in Columbia Tower, she invited him to visit the property on Thursday. He agreed.

At his desk, he started going through the stack of files his boss Sybil had given him that morning. She'd attached Post-it notes to each file—handwritten in a neat, almost archaic backhand, the kind he would expect to find on some sorority invitation dictated by the unspoken rules of class—as if being chosen wasn't determined by the size of a client's account spit out on computer paper from a database.

When she had brought the files to his office, she'd tossed her long silk scarf over one shoulder rather flamboyantly and, explaining that she was in a hurry, glanced out the window with a momentary hint of panic in her eyes. She dropped the files onto his desk, her bangle bracelets clanging like cymbals.

If she were part of any sorority, Garret mused, it was the sisterhood of the upwardly mobile. She was, above all, a survivor.

"Let me know, Garret, when you have questions on these." She sighed in such a way he couldn't help feeling she was unloading a burden on him.

Of course she wasn't inviting questions now, Garret thought as he browsed through the files. That would happen when she could plug him into a neat slot in her calendar after she had prepped herself.

His window overlooked the waterfront and he watched as the clouds slowly separated, the beginnings of the sunset glowing along the horizon, the view reminding him of his flight into the city only four days before.

The pilot, speaking in a mild southern accent with a hint of military authority, had jarred Garret out of a light nap when he announced the landing into Seattle. Garret thought the plane jerked into a descent too soon, but everything lately felt like it was happening too quickly. His life over the past month had felt abrupt: rushing to Seattle for a job interview and accepting the offer, resigning suddenly from his job in Chicago, leaving his family and friends behind.

It had been abrupt, but he hoped it didn't imply he was running away, and that any minor misunderstandings could be mended. Couldn't they? In the plot line of his life, he tended to burn his bridges. And he didn't really know why.

The plane descended below the clouds and he saw the Cascade Mountains clearly—layers and layers of mountains. Most were snow-covered, with more mountains than he had imagined you could see all at once.

"Folks, I have to tell ya," the pilot said, sounding almost gleeful. "This is the clearest view of Puget Sound we've had all winter. On both sides of the plane is the Cascade mountain range and those of you on the left will be able to see Mt. Rainier."

Garret looked out beyond the wing and there it was. He'd seen photos, but this was incredible: a single huge mountain, almost completely covered in snow, its peak sparkling in the sunlight above a thin mist as if it were detached from the ground below.

As they continued their descent he saw clusters of suburbs, some small lakes, Lake Washington, and Puget Sound—a huge expanse of water dotted with islands in every direction. And to the west was yet another range of snow-capped mountains that covered his entire view—the Olympics.

People he knew who'd been to Seattle had raved about the views—like his long-time high school buddy Vance. He'd been curious to see if the views were really all that. But his first flight into the city for the job interviews had arrived in the fog.

The pilot cleared his throat, as if still in awe himself. "Take a good long look around folks, 'cause this is it. This is God's country."

From his office window, off to the left, Garret could see enormous waterfront elevators that could lift an entire train car or truck cab. Imports—electronics mostly, and goods of all sorts—were constantly arriving in swarms of boxes from Asia, off ships from Vancouver, and from the East. Out to his right he could see tour boats, shops, and restaurants spread out along numbered piers.

"Dude? Hey, what's up?"

His buddy's voice brought him out of his daydream and he turned toward the door. "Vance! This is a surprise!" They gave each other a hug and some skin.

"Told you I'd pop in soon as I could." Vance shook his head as he looked past Garret towards the window. "Man, you've got the set-up with this view!"

"I'm tellin' ya! The waterfront, the ships, the ferries comin' in. Say man, you're lookin' good. Lookin' pretty fit."

"Not really, me? You're the one! That's a sharp suit, man. I see working here is no casual affair."

"Well no, not when I have to show up to meetings with clients. But my philosophy is, if I don't have outside meetings I can show up in comfortable stuff and keep it laid back."

"Hey, you gotta be your own boss no matter what." He nodded approvingly. He walked around the side of Garret's desk, sizing up the office and noticing the pictures on top of his bookshelf. "Nice picture of your family. And Jackie? How old is that picture?"

"It's pretty old. It was packed in with the stuff from my old office. I don't know if I should, you know, have it here. Or maybe just start fresh …"

"Man, whatever feels right. She's still part of you, right?"

Garret nodded, not sure how to describe the way he felt about Jackie now. "So how's Nadine?"

"Oh she's great, just a little overworked is all. She's so full of energy, wants to be all things to all people. Man, teaching in a high school? There's no such thing as ever being finished." Vance shook his head. "I just don't want to see her get burned out on her job and think it's me, know what I'm sayin'?" Garret nodded knowingly. "But we're gonna head for Hawaii together in October—that's the plan. It'll be my engagement present. So… you got some time to go down and grab a beer?"

Garret looked at the files on his desk and shrugged. "Sure thing. I just need to log off."

The walk down the hill to the waterfront was steep and quick.

"You know, Garret, I thought I was immune but I'm startin' to see what people are talkin' about with all this work-life balance b.s. Even now at Microsoft with all the early retirements, people are still trying to outdo the next guy in every department. All that, along with the added fixation on Y2K, means working late, stocking those refrigerators with microwave food, takin' a nap just to report back to work at 9 p.m. It's not for me. I told Nadine to look out for me when we moved in together, said I didn't want to turn into one of those work junkies. Now I'm the one trying to warn her about all the hours she's putting in—tutoring kids in the evenings, even trying to tutor parents. Man, now she's organizing SAT classes, too. She's that school's dream-come-true."

"What a lady! I wish I'd met somebody like her when I was in high school."

"I'm tellin' ya, I got lucky. And nobody can say no to that woman, least of all me. In fact, she's got me tutoring math at night. Can you believe it?" Vance looked at him, smiling.

"I'm real happy for you, dude," Garret said, patting him on the back.

They walked past some of the piers, past tour boats and restaurants selling deep-fried fish. An inviting scent of wood and burning charcoal mixed with the salty air and the sweet caramel aroma of candied apples.

"This place here has some microbrew, man." Vance nodded in the direction of a busy restaurant. They ordered from the outside window and sat on a picnic table on a big deck with small heaters suspended above them.

Garret felt a cooling mist drifting up from the water. "Sunset is really my favorite time of day. When I was in law school I'd be in the library studying, getting ready to quit for the day, but then I'd catch a glimpse of the sunset and it was like my brain switched on again."

"I know what you're sayin'. Especially out here. Like today—we didn't actually see the sun until now, until it got below the clouds. The sun is a big deal here. When it comes out, you have to jump on it. Like be ready for a bike ride, or whatever you been wantin' to do, or maybe just stare at it!" Vance chuckled.

"And everything looks so green!"

"Wait 'til you get over to the Olympics, to the rain forest and the old growth—you ain't seen nothin' like it. Nadine and I went out there last summer." Vance smiled. "That's when we decided to tie the knot."

Garret had never seen his buddy so smitten. Now he was really anxious to meet Nadine.

"You still up for Redman at Jazz Alley this Friday?" Vance asked him.

"You got it, man. I've got all his CDs, but I never heard him in person."

With the clouds clearing, the island across the way was more visible. Even from this distance he could see it was covered with evergreens. "You know man, I'm feeling good about this move—about startin' fresh, comin' to a place where it's not childhood associations or whatever that connects me, but the place itself. And imagining what it might have been like hundreds of years ago—before roads, before tall buildings. It must have been one heck of a big forest."

They sipped their brews and watched the water. The wide bronze patch of sunlight converted slowly to peach and then faded gently into a thin gold line.

After work, Ruthie headed to Pike Market to grab something quick to eat before her dance class. The market was bathed in a soft rose afterglow and soon the street lamps came on. A few produce stands were still open, their vendors shouting out closing time discounts. It was too bad that Arnie never had a chance to put in his garden the way he had planned, she thought, as she passed by asparagus and onions from Yakima. An employee with the agriculture department who didn't believe in pesticides, he was ahead of his time.

She had told him about her grandparents' place on Waldron Island in the San Juans. People from Seattle would *ooh* and *ah* about that kind of rustic living being idyllic, but the novelty of life without electricity could wear off during the short wet days of winter. There were only a few cars on the island, so people had to be their own mechanics or wait their turn. Growing up, Ruthie went every summer. Her grandfather had been a Mr. Fixit; both he and Grandma had spent dawn to dusk working on other people's gardens and then their own. But what Ruthie remembered best was the fresh produce—the strawberries and blackberries and apples, the filberts, the walnuts, and every vegetable you could think up. And their place was a real color fest for many months of the year, with all the flowers her grandmother had.

She remembered trailing blackberries, the kind people said were native, growing in low clumps that didn't invade the rest of the yard. In late summer it was always sunny and she'd be out picking berries, and they'd be warm and sweet and almost taste like wine. Exploring the island, she'd seen acres of wild roses—roses that turned out to be natives—and huge stands of oak trees that were rare in Washington, part of a prairie system that existed only in parts of the San Juan Islands and a few other places in the state. Collecting fallen acorns was just part of her life every summer, as she found little paths through the oaks.

As Ruthie waited in line in a deli at the edge of the market, she remembered one summer in particular. When she was eleven, right before Labor Day, she'd hidden in the woods for two hours when her mom came to pick her up to go back to school. The new shoes her mom tried to bribe her with felt too tight after going barefoot most of the summer. That's when she'd asked about the school on Waldron, but her mom wasn't having it. Ruthie had told Gran she had no interest in sixth grade, but she knew that if she let any tears show, Gran and Mom wouldn't be impressed. Gran told her the island wasn't going anywhere and neither were she and Gramps, and that there would be plenty of weekends and always the next summer. Finally, Ruthie had relented.

Thankfully, her parents had been neutral about college. They'd said that if she wanted to wait they wouldn't push it, and her grandparents had even said that she could live with them—work the farm, start a greenhouse, keep bees, do whatever she wanted. It had been tempting, and in hindsight she couldn't quite remember why she had chosen the University over Waldron, why she'd left to major in botany when it was all back there: every Northwest botany experiment a person could dream up could happen on those islands.

As a kid sitting under those trees, she felt like she had it all. She didn't have to prove herself to anyone. It was back there in the scent of apples that tasted like cider warming in the sun, back there in the bees collecting pollen, their legs bulging bright yellow, back there in the tulips and gladiolas and daffodils. She didn't need to be discovered by anyone, to perform for anyone. Back then, it was more about feelings than about words. And even then she knew the only person in the world who really had to accept her was herself.

Chapter Two

†

The next morning Garret walked from Belltown into downtown under a light drizzle, eventually folding up his umbrella as he walked under awnings and overhanging roofs.

Finally, he arrived at the base of Columbia Tower. The Starbucks inside looked crowded. As he was about to go in, a dark-skinned brother with short dreadlocks looked his way. "Spare some change?" the brother asked casually.

Garret felt into his pocket where he had a few coins. He was no fan of being weighed down by a lot of change.

"Gimme a chance, and I'll do a sun dance," the man added.

Garret remembered a woman in Chicago who would only accept dollar bills when she panhandled. The brother had a steady look that reminded Garret of his father, and so he set down his briefcase and reached for his wallet, trying to think of something that rhymed.

"I'm just a workin' dude with an attitude," Garret replied, pleased with himself. As he handed over a dollar, the guy leaned forward in a slight bow.

"Watch the dot-com bubble, it'll make you stumble," the guy countered, folding the dollar twice.

Garret smiled, picking up his briefcase. "Hope today's story is hunky dory," he said as he walked inside.

Back in Chicago he had friends who were rappers and he had found himself making beats on an MP3 beat machine to back them up. Some of them were pretty tight, but nobody could get it together enough to market the stuff.

When he got to the small office kitchen on his floor, Larry, another trust officer, was making coffee. Larry was the biggest producer on the team, and their boss Sybil had made a big deal about his six-month case total at the staff meeting. Garret nodded a greeting when he looked up.

"So guy, how's your apartment? Did you end up in Belltown?" Larry asked.

"For the time being. Till I get the neighborhoods figured out. The rent is a little pricey, but I like walking to work."

"Heck yes. The commute from the eastside is driving me totally nuts." Larry glanced over at the door and dropped his voice. "You know, I think Sybil may be taking some heat from the investment department. She told me some lawyer called one of the investment guys about one of our trusts—the Nielsen charitable trust. They sold a bunch of growth stock and they weren't supposed to. The beneficiary's only 45 and it wasn't supposed to start paying out till she retired."

That sounded like a big deal but Garret tried to keep his cool. "And they sold the stock already?"

"Yup. If they'd held on, those tech stocks would have split and multiplied like a goddamn barn full of rabbits. The beneficiary didn't notice the mistake 'cause it was her mother who set the thing up, but Mrs. Nielsen got furious and had her lawyer call Brad in the investment department. Now Brad's boss is saying we never gave them any direction."

"Was he off base about that?" Garret took two mugs out of the cupboard.

"These investment guys say they never got a trust memo for it. That's where they get their direction on investing." Larry took the pot off the stand and filled both mugs.

"So it was your trust?"

"You got it. That's what I'm a little uptight about—I can't remember if I wrote the memo or not, so if the shit hits the fan, they're either going to try and blame me or blame Sybil as my manager. 'Cause the deal is, she's supposed to sign off on those memos before they go to Investing."

Garret found some milk in the small fridge. "Every work situation I've been in is up against this type of blame throwing." Garret added some milk to his coffee and stirred it slowly. "I mean, you're the big producer in the office, so you may be in a rush once in awhile. Maybe you need some backup with paperwork, or some system that tracks these memos, but you more or less have to do contortions to get any kind of clerical support."

"Bingo. You know, ah… Sybil might ask you to go over the case, since you're a lawyer. And, well, you're fresh blood."

Garret sipped his coffee. Fresh blood? Did that mean there were vampires in the neighborhood? "When I was hired I didn't realize I'd be the only lawyer in the group."

"'Fraid so. The guy you replaced was a lawyer. Nancy's a CPA, Peter has an MBA—he's really more of a trainee like Georgia, anyway—and of course, Sybil. She's a banker. You know, started as a bank teller, worked her way up the ranks, and now every trust officer in town would love to have her plum job. And me, I'm just a poor ex-stock broker."

"Yeah? Then maybe you can make sense out of this client I have comin' in with stocks like Internap and F5 Networks. I never heard of these companies, and the dude said he wants to start a foundation with these stocks. What if the companies go bust?"

"That's what the minimum fee is about. I set up two foundations last year that are still just shells—they say they'll put money in eventually. And another client, I begged him to diversify—all he has is Microsoft. I suggested he at least convert to a few mutual funds, but the guy tells me that Microsoft, as a company, is more diverse than a mutual fund. You can't talk to these people."

Back at his desk, Garret checked his stack of files but didn't see anything on the Nielsen case. In Chicago he'd learned how to get loans to poor folks and how to help a few of the rich ones give some of their Benjamins away. He'd also learned that getting caught up in office politics was as toxic as drinking water out of Lake Erie.

On the way to his afternoon appointment, he stopped in a music store and found two Coltrane CDs to send to Arnie. One had "My Favorite Things" on it and the other was the album "A Love Supreme." He thought Rhea would probably like the first one, and he knew he couldn't miss with the second for Arnie; it was the most healing and spiritual music he could think of.

He headed up Pine Street past a guy with no teeth selling newspapers, past a Mayan band playing a South American tune he had played in college, past people of all ages with all hair colors, including orange and purple, past folks with midriffs revealing belly button rings and tattoos everywhere. He walked past two slender Asian girls wearing capris with thick high heels, each loaded down with big Nordstrom bags.

He passed the new Nordstrom store and a fancy espresso bar, and then came to Pacific Place, the elaborate four-story shopping center, with its Tiffany's—a store that symbolized New York and money. Jewelry was spaced perfectly under glass, lit with spotlights, alongside colored glass dishes that shined as if no speck of dust had ever entered the place.

Inside the shopping center, a clothing boutique had window displays featuring peacock and burgundy shawls draped over sweaters—suggesting sculpture more than clothing—at prices he could only imagine. The shops all looked busy. Folks were riding the escalators with their shopping bags full, or sitting in cafes in groups, leaning over espressos and decadent pastries like there was no tomorrow.

Madeleine Knight, who had been one of Sybil's clients, had picked Desert Fire, a restaurant located on the top level of Pacific Place. As he rode the escalator up he recognized the enticing aroma of salsa and spices and heard Latin music playing. Desert Fire—with its stucco walls and Southwest shades of gold, coral, and turquoise—seemed to be the antithesis of the Northwest. Small chalkboards described the snacks served during happy hour and listed Mexican beers. Apparently this was a spot where people could be transported to a place where everything was warm and dry. He picked a table next to the windows and took another look at Madeleine's file.

A flowery intoxicating scent crossed his nostrils and as he looked up, he saw a woman. Probably in her early thirties, she was younger than he'd expected. Madeleine Knight. She was a little plump, with layered blondish hair that rippled to her shoulders, and thick lips which she emphasized with shiny pink lipstick that matched her jacket. He got up quickly and shook her hand, trying to make a gesture toward her chair but the waiter beat him to it.

She sat across from him, leaning in as she spoke. "So Garret, are you sweet or are you savory?" As she moved, the silver gray of her pearl earrings and necklace sparkled in the subdued light of the amber-colored fixtures overhead.

He drew a blank, and then realized she was talking about the menu.

"I was thinking about mushroom quesadillas, but those miniature tamales look tasty," she added.

"Well, how about we try a plate of each? We can share. And a couple of Mexican beers?"

"Perfect! Garret, I really appreciate you meeting me this late, since I have to be downtown tonight."

The waiter reappeared and they ordered the food and some Coronas.

"So, I've gone over your file, and I want to make sure you've been satisfied with the performance of the trust."

She nodded. "It's done well. I'm just trying to decide where to go next. I'd really like more diversification, if I could figure a way out of all the capital gains taxes."

The waiter returned and poured their beers into tall chilled glasses.

"I don't know if it's just me, but it's really warm in here." Slowly, she unbuttoned the pearl buttons of her jacket. A bit ceremoniously, he thought.

Her blouse was a thin translucent silver gray material that revealed the outline of her bra, which was made of a shiny fabric, and her pearl necklace hung just above the line of satin and into her cleavage. She turned slowly sideways to put the jacket over the back of her chair, and the V-neck of her blouse opened, revealing the top of her breasts.

He could feel something stir in the pit of his groin. Maybe, he thought, Madeleine was the sort of woman he could have fun with, without getting serious. She looked like a very sensuous woman, a woman who would take her time in bed. The way she moved, it felt as if she had time to draw things out. Her sensuality wasn't subtle, he thought. But it wasn't gauche, either.

She crossed her legs and somehow the V of her blouse dropped lower so that he could see a lot of cleavage. He was beginning to feel a mild dizziness, an intoxication that was better than booze or drugs, and he hadn't even tasted the beer yet. If they were on a date, he could stare freely at her boobs. He could give her that steady gaze that meant there would be something to follow. They'd proceed to a place where they would dance, and he could put his hand on her soft round butt, and hold her in his arms to make sure she liked it. He enjoyed the prelims as much as any other part of the connection with a woman.

The waiter brought the plates of food.

"Oh, these look yummy," she said, sliding a couple of each on her plate. "Maybe what I need is to set up a foundation as an outlet for some of the stock."

He had never imagined software engineers as sensuous or glamorous, and had been prepped that these software retirees often showed up in jeans and sweatshirts. She was the sort of woman he could have fun with all right—with one important exception. She was a client. He needed to pull himself together.

He took a sip of beer and forced himself to stare down at the file again. "I was looking over some of the work from the tax department, and I think a foundation would be a good fit. Of course, there is the issue of the stock options, which will require some more tax research. And this is assuming you have some charitable interests?"

"Of course. Doesn't everybody?"

He shook his head. "Not really." He felt like saying that most people don't have the bucks to be philanthropic.

"It's just a matter of choosing the most important charities. I'm interested in a lot of things—the arts, education, the environment—mostly local things."

His brow was sweating slightly. "Well, we can help you. Sometimes I do charity site visits. Not that I'm going to suggest what to give to, but I can help you develop some benchmarks for measuring success."

She smiled as if her whole psyche were locked into the present. He noticed her eyes were an unusual shade of light gray, almost the same color as her pearls. He took out his handkerchief and wiped his brow. Rarely had he been so attracted to a client. He watched as she picked up a quesadilla, part of her shiny bra reflecting the light. Her look was so direct it was hard to imagine that this wasn't an open invitation.

He took a few bites and stared at the file again. He couldn't allow himself to be tricked; he knew how powerful a sexual urge could be. It could undermine anything, any well-laid plan. He wondered if his boss had referred Madeleine to him as a test. It was a cold thought, but Sybil wasn't born yesterday. Fortunately, neither was he.

"Well, the financial statements look good," he told her. "Are you considering any business ventures or any other need for capital, like a house purchase?"

"I'm thinking of investing in a theater over on the Eastside with a couple of partners, maybe going in with around two million in stock."

"Okay, then I would say you and I should meet with your CPA as our next step."

"Sounds like a good plan, Garret," she said smiling, slowly sipping her beer. "I'm sure you two will make a great team."

Ruthie had to work late so she walked over to Westlake Mall to grab some dinner at the food court. On the ground level, a woman was installing a large spotlight in a display window in front of The Limited, a clothing store Ruthie rarely set foot in. The bright light was pointed toward a large poster of a male model that sent chills up her spine. For a split second she didn't know why. Sure, the young model was inordinately handsome, with dark brown hair cut into uneven spikes, huge hazel eyes, somewhat chiseled features, and dressed in an alluring black turtleneck. But then she realized what it was. His face bore a stunning resemblance to Fioretti, her first big crush.

His full name was Cameron Fioretti, but everyone just called him Fioretti. She was in eleventh grade when she was hot for him—too unsophisticated to know even what hotness might fully entail. His parents had come from Italy only a couple of years before and both taught at the U.W. For awhile, his social sphere seemed totally impenetrable.

He dressed in thin silk shirts with his collar open to the middle of his chest, invariably revealing a gold chain that suggested something quintessentially sexual. He was wiry and claimed not to like team sports, although his body possessed a unique compact muscle tone which he reluctantly attributed to running and playing soccer. A tinge of an Italian accent heightened his appeal. But the more she learned about him, the more she realized that what really set him apart was not that he wasn't a jock or an American; it was that he was an intellectual.

She had struggled through Camus and Sartre in French class, fumbling through the dictionary frequently and resorting to the English translation when she was desperate, while Fioretti had read them—entirely in French—for pleasure. He told her that his mother had read the whole *Iliad* aloud to him when he was eight, and he explained that he was generally satisfied with earning only Bs in school so he had time to read and study what he wanted. He wrote poetry, loaded with double meanings, for the school literary magazine, including one called "Organisms," a coded description of what it felt like to have a sexual climax. Ruthie couldn't resist his intense stares during English class, those penetrating eyes, his olive skin, his toned body.

An acquaintance of Ruthie's named Isabelle was hooked up in Fioretti's crowd, and so Ruthie decided there was no harm in getting to know Isabelle better. After school one day, she invited her to go to the university district to hang out in the Hub, the campus student union, which she figured was one of Isabelle's regular haunts anyway. Isabelle had told her about a guy she was seeing, a friend of Fioretti's, and leaked that Fioretti had asked her about Ruthie. After a little more go-between action, Ruthie went on her first date with Fioretti.

He came to pick her up with a guy named Whitman, who drove a van with two seats in front and only a mattress in back. That mattress was an ominous beginning to their series of encounters.

One evening, they went together to a prom called May Dance. And although Fioretti had made no pretensions about being the prom type, even warning her that his wallet was too thin for the customary after-prom steakhouse dinner, he arrived at Ruthie's door with the most gorgeous orchid corsage she had ever seen.

He was low-key on the dance floor, openly resisting the up-tempo stuff that pumped up most of the crowd, but Ruthie didn't mind. They danced to some slow songs, his thumb touching the bare part of her back giving her a tingling sensation. Even at May Dance Fioretti had assembled a couple of his friends who quipped about the function but egged on the band since, it turned out, Whitman was the lead singer.

After the dance and a snack of tea and cinnamon toast at a café near campus, he took her home, satisfied it seemed with a reasonably long make-out session. But it wasn't long before Fioretti made some more moves.

The next week-end they were with Whitman and his current girlfriend in the front of the van. Even though Ruthie was still smitten with Fioretti, when the other couple started going at it and Fioretti tried to unhook her bra, she mumbled, "not now." He sighed loudly and pulled away. Whitman turned around and asked, "What's the story?"

Fioretti explained that he had to get up early and needed to go home, so Whitman restarted the engine, fuming to himself.

After they dropped her off, Ruthie fantasized that Fioretti would come to the door later and tell her it was okay if she wanted to wait on the sexual thing, that sex wasn't even all that important. He didn't come back. But as she waited, her fantasies became more complex: She might run into him down at the boathouse on campus, and he'd take her out in a canoe and tell her that whatever she wanted was fine, that there was an undeniable magnetism between them and that the sexual thing would work itself out in time.

Weeks later, when she went to a student art show, she saw a woodcut that reminded her of him: an abstract painting of a rosebush, thorns and all. "A rose in bloom pollutes the air," he had said to her once. She bought the woodcut and hung it at the foot of her bed in her bright yellow room; it looked out of place there, but her mother didn't say anything.

Looking at it hanging there had reminded her of other things he had said, too: the night she was babysitting and he came by for a short visit, asking "What is more natural, sex or breathing?" She wasn't able to answer. Maybe her mother had been right. Maybe she was a late bloomer.

Suddenly, Ruthie noticed that the woman in the display case was watching her. How long had she been standing there, staring at the poster?

Ruthie smiled, blushing, and nodded toward the picture of the male model, as if to suggest that she might be some sort of fashion critic or a connoisseur of hunks. Looking at the poster more closely, she realized that being reminded of Fioretti probably had more to do with his calling her last week—asking her to have dinner with him while he was visiting Seattle—than with any real resemblance to the model.

It had been out of the blue. Almost. When he called, he said he wasn't trying to rekindle an old flame, just reconnect as an old friend. She had to go for that; an adult conversation that wasn't laced with her unrequited sexual obsession seemed reasonable. The best thing she could do for her mental health was to not ruminate about the guy, and no exploitive ad was going to trigger passé memories of her sixteen-year-old hormones. Not for long, anyway.

She grabbed a sandwich and got her act back to the office.

Chapter Three

†

On Thursday Garret saw the brother with the short locks again, standing in front of the bank building with a stack of newspapers. "If you're not lame, you'll read Real Change," he said, gesturing to the paper he was holding as Garret approached.

Garret didn't recognize the paper, but there was a picture of a homeless tent city on the front. It seemed like a good cause, so he reached into his wallet for a buck. "I'll give it a shot, I kid you not," he managed.

The guy hesitated, but only for a second. "Don't be found when they make their rounds, we'll never know for sure who snuffed Shakur," talking about Tupac. The guy was quick.

Garret hesitated, letting the traffic noise around him serve as a beat.

"When the streets are mean, it's a random scene."

The guy gave him a thumb's up and handed him the paper, adding, "Keep it real, brother, keep it real."

He kept the beat in his head as he walked into the building. He took the elevator to the garage, picked up the bank's Honda, and drove to Ruthie's office near Westlake Mall. She was already waiting out front when he pulled up.

"Hey Garret!" she said as she jumped in the passenger side. "I have great hopes for today. It's the first day in months that I've seen morning sun!"

"Yeah? Somebody at the bank said his neighbor from California moved back 'cause it's been such a long winter," he said as he eased back into traffic.

"Yeah, this winter has pushed the envelope."

"Well, it's milder than Chicago."

She shook her head and smiled, giving him a look that might have meant 'just you wait till you make it through an entire winter.'

As they got on the freeway and passed the university district, traffic started thinning out, and Garret glanced over at her. "You said the Conservancy has lots of land up on the Skagit?"

"Yeah, we own over a thousand acres. But we're part of a huge effort with all these public agencies, so altogether we're protecting over ten thousand. And this buffers North Cascades National Park."

"Impressive. There's a woman at the bank who told me she's been on one of those eagle trips up there. She sounded just like Arnie when she talked about it."

"Well, you've got yourself an invitation for next January to see huge flocks of eagles from Alaska." Then she added, almost as if she thought she had sounded too forward, "We take lots of groups up in January. It's really cold, but it's awesome."

The evergreens along the freeway thickened as they approached the city of Lynnwood, about fifteen miles north of Seattle proper. Ruthie told him about the Scotch broom in the middle of the freeway and how you needed a special weed wrench to dig them out. Near Everett they stopped for lattes, and then cruised through some farmland that was almost marshy. Occasional barns and farmhouses were clustered together. Cattle grazed on patches like in the Midwest except it was hilly and there were creeks and small streams everywhere.

"Tulip country," she pointed out.

"Everything is on such a grand scale out here," he told her. "We used to go camping quite a bit in Illinois and up in the lakes of northern Wisconsin, though there were places my dad wouldn't go—rural places where you wouldn't see black people at all. You know, my dad's black and my mom's white." Ruthie nodded, perhaps as a gesture for him to keep talking.

"She grew up there and was more or less used to it," he continued, "but my dad, he wouldn't go into the little towns up in the north woods where you had to take your chances. Up in those towns you never knew what kind of hang-ups somebody might have about mixed marriages or whatever, and a lot of them were into duck hunting and drinking a lot. So my brother and I did a lot of camping just with my mom. I taught myself to fish and I kind of dug that for awhile." He paused for a moment and cleared his throat. "But I actually grew up thinking my dad didn't want to be with us on those trips. I took the whole thing personally."

"When it was really more about prejudice," she said.

He nodded tentatively. Yes, he thought, it was mostly that. Or partly that, and also other things: the unique peculiarities of each parent's desire, perhaps, just to be in charge, however briefly, during what might otherwise have been a stressful family vacation. He had learned over time that both of his parents tended to be reclusive, but in different ways. And he had come to realize that they didn't always want to be reclusive together.

But he wasn't going to try and describe his parents' relationship to someone he had just met on a business trip, even someone as sympathetic as Ruthie. After all, he had drafted a success script for himself, and that script said that he was to appear functional and dynamic at all times—at work and anywhere else for that matter. Still the rich green countryside rushing past reminded him of being a kid and going on those trips.

Once, when he was about ten, someone had called him the *n* word at the lake in one of his favorite state parks. His mom had been more upset by it than he was, and when another kid took his side they both ganged up on the punk. After they ran the kid out of the lake, his mom told him that people who make bigoted remarks usually do it because they're so insecure about themselves. And he told her, "Duh." He'd forgotten the incident until she reminded him of it once when he was home from college.

When he was a kid he was at the center of the universe and no one could really get in his way. In high school and later in college, even when people seemed to expect to see it, the race card wasn't the first one he pulled out of his vest pocket. The cards he held close to his chest said things like 'Be Cool', and pictured someone like Miles Davis, whose very existence was the definition of taking no shit, or 'Hang Tight', featuring a hip hop artist like André from OutKast.

Besides. As a kid, he didn't just watch "The Cosby Show." He became a fan of "In Living Color," and the irrepressible imagination of Daman Wayans when he constructed "This Old Box," a cardboard version of "This Old House."

As they left I-5 and took the road toward Darrington the clouds and fog began to clear, revealing the enormous face of a snow-covered mountain that seemed so close it filled Garret's entire range of vision.

"White Horse Mountain," Ruthie told him as his eyes widened.

Not long after, they glimpsed the Sauk River with its large gravel bars and logjams. The river was a tributary of the Skagit, she said, pointing out the slender sedate cottonwoods lazily adjoining the curve of the river. Their slate green leaves were almost silver, glinting in slow motion like mirrors as their lean trunks shifted in a gentle breeze—resilient, undisturbed, carefree and wild.

On the outskirts of the town of Rockport, they passed a state park and the road ran up against the Skagit River—

with water that was forest green and wide and speedy like the Mississippi. Bright white sheets of fog sparkled over the water, slowly separating, revealing mountains that covered the entire landscape.

"Every time I come up here and see the river and the mountains, life feels big and important and beautiful. Even in the rain," she added. "And in the sun, well, just wait until you see it. People say the Skagit is the crown jewel of the Northwest and they're right."

The road wove in and out of forested landscapes and back and forth along the river. On the left were abandoned looking farms and more old trucks and cars than Garret had ever seen and then they passed a sign that said "Welcome to Marblemount. Entrance to the American Alps." Just beyond the sign was an old house with carved wooden statues of deer, beaver, and bear splayed around the yard.

The neon sign of a bar flickered "Bar is Open," with brands of beer lit up and blinking alongside it.

"Last Beer for 89 Miles," he read out loud from the hand-painted sign.

Ruthie laughed. "Yup. It's a long way through the mountains to Winthrop."

After passing a restaurant, a gas station, and a grocery store, they came to the bridge that crossed the Skagit. Clouds streamed over the tops of the mountains like smoke, obscuring the faces of wet rock and narrow stands of trees that intersected large jagged clear-cuts sloped along the mountain crevices.

They took a right turn toward another bridge crossing the Cascade River, which seemed even louder and speedier than the Skagit, with long gravel bars and a section that gushed sideways in rapids so rough that the river resembled moving rock more than it did water. And then he realized he really hadn't spent much time in mountains at all. He'd been skiing in Colorado a few times, but here… These rivers were rushing out of the mountains and had somewhere to go—eventually, he guessed, out to saltwater in Puget Sound.

Evergreens lined both sides of the road. "This is all second growth," Ruthie told him, gesturing at a stand of trees. "The timber company speeded up their logging knowing that a bird—the Marbled Murrelet—was going on the endangered species list."

After a small clearing they came to a narrow dirt road marked "private" that headed toward the water. Turning right, they saw more driveways and stopped at the third one. It was marked "McGowan," with a large yellow gate across the gravel driveway.

They parked outside the gate. Garret thought it was strange that Arnie had given them all the keys except the one for the gate, but it was padlocked and evidently the son-in-law had the only key. So they found their way around the gate through brambles.

Ruthie tried a couple of keys on the garage door and finally opened it. The structure was just a frame with a dirt floor and a few tools and wood inside. Beyond it was a wide trail that seemed to bisect the property, covered mostly in moss and wet gravel and some of the biggest ferns he had ever seen, and trees draped in delicate pale green lichen hanging still in the moist heavy air, weighted motionless by the mists of time.

They walked along the trail between large stands of cedars and Doug firs, many with trunks covered in moss.

"This place feels so complete," she said. "Like there's room for everything to grow."

At the end of the trail they came to a steep bank.

"Wow," Ruthie said, gesturing to a place further ahead. "See this gravel path here, that switchbacks down to the river? That has to be new. When I was here before, it didn't even go down the high bank to the river."

"Looks to me like it took a heck of a lot of work to put all this gravel in here. And Arnie didn't mention that boathouse there when he gave you those keys."

"Oh, that wasn't here either," she said. "I would have remembered that."

They made their way down the slippery gravel path. The boathouse was raised up on blocks. The door wasn't locked, though there was a metal strip and hook for a padlock.

"I thought they usually put windows in these things," he said as Ruthie opened the door to let some light into the building.

"Yeah. You'd be hard pressed to see anything in here with this door closed."

It looked empty inside.

Thin strands of gravel lined the water, and across the river was a huge gravel bar.

She pulled out her binoculars and pointed to the left at a spot a fair distance down the river, where he could see the white heads of a pair of eagles perched motionless, high in one of the bare trees. She handed him the binoculars.

"There are a couple of nests along this section of the river. But basically they've gone back to Alaska now to nest."

With the binoculars pressed against his eyes, Garret grinned. "I really haven't seen eagles sitting still before. They're awesome!" he said enthusiastically and Ruthie smiled.

When the eagles finally retreated back into the woods, Garret and Ruthie found their way back to the trail and headed back through the woods.

"Arnie was pretty savvy, in his way," she said, ducking under some branches. "See where that little clearing is on the other side of the garage? That's where he put his cabin." Garret nodded and they headed toward it.

The cabin looked nearly new, with a cache for rain and even a little outdoor shower. It had two built-in bunk beds large enough to sleep two each, sleeping bags rolled up neatly in a corner, a picnic table, and a wooden counter with a propane stove and some stools.

"Garret, this stove looks brand new!"

"Everything looks pretty new to me. It's not the typical old cabin kind of place. There's barely any dust in here."

"I think I see what Arnie was talking about. He said they hardly got a chance to use this place." She sat down on a stool, her eyes cast down at nothing in particular. "You know, I've never dealt with a land donation that was so…" She paused.

"Tragic?"

She nodded.

"Well, Ruthie, I haven't been through too many of these either, but I don't think Arnie is asking you to shed tears for him. He's asking you to do something larger than life—something he can't do alone and probably something his family wouldn't do without him. If he didn't want your organization to preserve the property, he wouldn't have turned those keys over to you. So, it looks to me like this donation of land could be one of the things in his life he's the most proud of."

She nodded and her eyes brightened. "How did you get so smart?"

She stood up, stretching her arms into the air with her hands folded together the way his ex-girlfriend Jackie used to do when she was learning yoga.

"Instead of getting maudlin," she added, "I guess the right thing for me to do now is help him get this donation done before he dies."

"Amen, sister," he said, patting her on the shoulder. "And this place is going to become more valuable by the minute."

Using a small camera he had brought for the job, he started taking pictures of the cabin.

They drove back through Rockport, past the state park, and started losing elevation quickly, staying on the highway until they reached the town of Mount Vernon.

"Here's the turnoff, Garret, if you still want to check out our little office. It's not much but it gives us a base of operations up here."

They took the exit and pulled up in front of a small strip mall with a copy place, a computer supply shop, and an insurance office.

Inside the office was a small reception area with a display of brochures and a large wall map of the Skagit River. A balding man with a white handlebar mustache appeared, a twinkle in his brilliant blue eyes.

"Garret, this is Roy, our Skagit land steward."

Garret shook his hand. "Good to meet you. It's awesome work you all are doing up here."

"Thanks," Roy said, a smile below his thick mustache. "It keeps us on our toes. We've just installed our GIS system. If you two have a minute I'll show you what we're up to. It's wild stuff."

"GIS?" Garret asked.

"Yeah, our Geographic Information System. We use it to do map layering."

They followed him into a cubicle with a computer and large color monitor.

"You can use these map layers to illustrate almost anything," he said, waving a hand towards the monitor. "Forests, salmon spawning areas, ownership, nesting areas for listed bird species, conservation status… you name it. Here's one," he said, typing something into the system. "It shows all the government agencies that are protecting various parcels of land on the Skagit. They're all shown in green."

Garret studied the screen. "Ruthie said the Forest Service stopped cutting along the river. How did you convince them of that?"

"I think folks up here are starting to get the idea that most of the Puget Sound salmon spawn up here and they need the trees to keep the system intact. Of course I'm biased, but if you ask me, Seattle's incomplete without the Skagit."

"I'm getting that impression myself," Garret told him.

"Roy, you see this parcel right here?" Ruthie pointed to a spot on the screen and he nodded. "Garret and I are working on getting that donated."

"Way to go!" His eyes sparkled. "That's where some of the biggest trees on this stretch are left. In the long run, it'll be places like this where we need examples of old growth so they can be replicated in larger public forests—eventually as a way of storing carbon."

"Is that like carbon sequestration?"

"Exactly. Did you say you work for a bank?" Garret nodded, and Roy smiled. "I didn't know bankers were so enlightened."

"Garret's the exception." Ruthie winked at him. She had primed him with some articles on the topic, but he didn't mind looking smart.

Before they got back on the road Ruthie used one of the office computers to check her email and Garret checked his voice mail. He had a couple of new messages including one, coincidentally, from Arnie McGowan's son-in-law, the lawyer. He sounded like he was in a hurry so Garret dialed him up. He answered on the second ring.

"Hello, Dan? This is Garret Carter from the bank. I just listened to your message. What can I do for you?"

"Hi there. Say, I got a call from Arnie's CPA and he said he wanted to see some numbers on this annuity deal."

"Sure, no problem. I've got those spreadsheets in the office. I'm not there right now, but I can fax them to you and the CPA first thing in the morning."

"Well, this material you sent me, it had Arnie down as a lifetime beneficiary along with Rhea."

"Having both of them as beneficiaries is an option if you wanted to signal to Arnie that you expect him to go into remission." He looked over at Ruthie, who was chatting with Roy in front of the computer.

Dan cleared his throat, taking his time. "But then the tax deduction would be smaller," he said in a patronizing, almost bored tone.

"Well, a little smaller, yes." Garret wasn't sure what Dan was getting at, but he was starting to get the impression Dan wasn't a hundred percent behind the land deal. "It's a family decision, of course. But either way you structure it, you'll see there are income and tax benefits either to Rhea or to both of them for their lifetimes." Garret took a breath. "And it's a great gift to conservation no matter what—a cause anyone can feel good about, don't you think?"

"Well, I never said we should give it to the Caucasian Nations." He was still using a near monotone, almost as if he were repeating prepared remarks.

The Caucasian Nations? Garret paused, wondering if he heard the guy right. The racist hate group? Where did that come from?

He took a deep breath. "Well, no… you never said that." Was this guy putting him on? Was this supposed to be his idea of humor to provoke someone of African descent?

"I mean if we're just talking *causes* … those guys need rifles too, just like anybody else."

This guy was really out of pocket. Garret cleared his throat and took another breath, working harder on trying to keep his cool.

Working for years in Chicago—making loans to low income people, plenty of black folks, working with all types of investors—

he had prepared himself for racial backlash. And sure, there had been letters and phone calls from people who represented hate groups or were just plain twisted, trying to bash the bank for setting up loan programs for minority businesses. But he had never been confronted directly in the middle of a transaction. And with those loans having one of the highest payback rates in the country, the hate mongers had no leg to stand on.

He pulled himself together. "I tell you what, man. I'll fax you the spreadsheets tomorrow morning and then I think we should set up a meeting with the CPA. I have a ride to catch." He pushed "End" without waiting for a response and slammed his fist against the inkpad on Roy's desk. "Damn!"

"Garret, what's wrong?" Ruthie rushed over to him.

"Arnie's son-in-law just delivered some serious bullshit over the phone. I'm just glad it didn't happen in person." He relayed the whole conversation, Ruthie's eyes growing wider as he talked.

Roy walked up just as Garret was finishing the story. "Man, I couldn't help overhearing. He sounds like a four-star asshole."

Ruthie shook her head and sighed in agreement. "You know, Garret, there are wackos everywhere. But it sounds as if you handled him beautifully."

"That's right, man," Roy added. "This Caucasian Nations is a serious white supremacist group over in northern Idaho, though I heard they were going broke."

"Well, this guy acted like he's a sympathizer. Arnie or Rhea must have said something about me to him."

"It sounds that way, Garret," Ruthie put in. "It blows my mind, though, especially since Arnie seemed so taken with you. He probably said great things about you and got Dan pissed off. Even jealous."

"Maybe he resents the whole idea of this donation to begin with," Roy added. "If his wife inherited the property from her parents instead, that would mean major bucks in their pockets, right?"

"True. I s'pose both of those are possibilities," Garret conceded. He shook his head. "Heck, I need to be prepared for any type of behavior. Dan may even be feeling a little over his head. This type of deal—exchanging land for an annuity—well, he's probably never heard of anything like this. They don't teach much of this stuff in law school."

"If he even remembers law school," Roy said.

"Remember when we met with Arnie?" Garret looked over at Ruthie. "He said he'd have his son-in-law take a quick look at the paperwork. I never got the impression from Arnie it was supposed to be a To Give or Not To Give debate."

"Me neither. We don't have time to start from scratch, considering how sick Arnie is," Ruthie said.

"Ok, here's the thing. I'll get another trust officer to take over. That way the son-in-law won't have any excuse to sabotage the deal over some sort of racial b.s." Garret was willing to do whatever it took to save the deal, but Ruthie and Roy both shook their heads.

"No way, man," Roy told him.

"Heck no. We're not going to cave in to that kind of pathetic behavior," Ruthie added. "You're our designated hitter on this deal. If the son-in-law can't behave himself, we'll talk to Arnie and ask him to appoint another lawyer."

This time Ruthie patted Garret on the shoulder. "I guess we're both getting tested on this one."

Chapter Four

†

Back in his apartment that evening, Garret opened some boxes that he still hadn't unpacked. In one was a framed photo of Jackie on a boat in Lake Michigan taken the day they'd gone for a sailing lesson.

She had her hair all blown out into an Afro, and she'd been out in the sun a lot and looked bronzed and vital. They had fun picking up a few pointers about sailing that day—the same day she told him she got a fellowship to go to grad school at the University of Michigan. It had come as a shock to him, but she said the program would go quickly, that they wouldn't be apart too long.

"I don't want you to go, but you gotta do it," he had said. He'd known it was a great opportunity, and if she turned it down because of their relationship, she might even blame him later. Besides, they weren't going to be that far apart.

They managed to stay in touch pretty well, got together for holiday breaks and long weekends. She was a good communicator, considering how busy she was. They talked a lot on the phone, exchanged e-mails, and went back and forth between Ann Arbor and Chicago for two years.

He set the picture on one of his bookshelves and fixed himself a sandwich.

That night he dreamed about Jackie. She was wearing her white coat, coming out of the door of the hospital where she worked. He was waiting for her in a rental car he'd picked up at the airport, and she was carrying a huge file that looked like someone's medical records, which she tossed into the backseat angrily.

"These chronic pain patients bailed on me," she said, fuming. "I spent three weeks working night and day, putting together a boss treatment plan. I had two MDs involved, a physical therapist, occupational therapist—a complete team. And these patients—they needed the treatment all right. A man and wife together. They didn't call, didn't cancel, they just bailed. Bailed for no reason other than I'm black." He'd never seen her pull out the race card before, but her eyes brimmed with tears.

He took her in his arms, but before he had a chance to give her a real hug, she faded away.

He woke up in a cold sweat and looked at the clock. Only 4:00 a.m. The stark glowing red digits of the clock almost seemed to vibrate. Why didn't he buy something subtler, something that glowed in the dark but didn't glare out at him like a visual fire alarm?

Damn, he thought. This was the first time in a month that he'd dreamed about her.

He tried to relax, to talk himself back to sleep. She'd been good at helping him relax, Jackie had, at least when she finally gave herself permission to slow down. She used to massage his tense back and tell him there was nothing that could hold him down, that he could do anything in the world he wanted to do. He had always liked the way her voice sounded soothing without sounding phony. It was part of the reason he knew she'd make a great psychologist.

He closed his eyes, clinically relaxing each muscle, trying to decide what he should do about the jerk son-in-law, Dan. The last thing he wanted now was for his first major deal to go south.

Sybil could present a mild exterior but she would evaluate him on his bottom line like any other boss. He knew he shouldn't waste his time trying to psychoanalyze some guy with a serious attitude problem like the one Dan obviously had. If he had wanted to do that, he would have become a psychologist like Jackie. He had a job to do and if a client wanted to make a charitable donation, that was his right. If a relative decided to sabotage the deal, well, he had to let the chips fall where they may and move on to another deal. That was the professional way to handle it.

He tried to clear his mind and he shifted on the mattress, trying to relax. He told himself that coming to Seattle had been the right thing to do, the right way to start fresh. A new leaf. Seattle could become his place now, if he stayed positive. When Sybil was recruiting him, she said it was a great opportunity for him to break into the new philanthropy, referring to software millionaires and new dot-com business owners.

Sybil told him that when she first came to Seattle in the early seventies, Seattle was like a big country town. All these individual neighborhoods and a pretty small financial district. But not now. Now there was major money in the city and over on the Eastside and the bank wanted to be the number one go-to to manage it. The bank wanted in, and his experience with younger, more diverse clients could bring in some new business, she said. She told him about one of her clients, a software engineer and millionaire many times over whose family had been sharecroppers. Everything was new now. As much as her comment hinted at a corporate brand of tokenism, it had sounded plausible. After all, some of the software millionaires weren't much older than he was and they certainly didn't represent old money.

By 5:30 it was obvious he wouldn't be falling back to sleep. He got up and made some strong coffee, packed his work-out bag, and headed over to the gym.

He got on the treadmill and managed to work up a decent sweat. He liked the view from the windows out onto Third and the sight of the neighborhood waking up—folks dressed in office clothes stepping off of buses, the traffic picking up, a few homeless people buying coffee in the deli—coming to life.

He did some bench presses and free weights. If he could get to the gym a few times a week, he figured he'd build himself up to handle the weight he'd been able to bench in college.

By the time he was a block from his office building he felt wired. He started to cross the street but somebody in a BMW stopped him, cutting him off even though he had a walk sign. As he waited for the light to change again, he noticed the dude with short dreadlocks selling the Real Change paper in front of his building.

As he watched, an older white guy with a backpack grabbed the brother's money from his coffee can and took off. Garret was stunned. He crossed the street quickly.

He was sure the dude must have noticed the guy rip him off, but when Garret got there the dude just looked toward him and said, "Around every corner they're pushin' hate, lurkin' nearby and in my face, I got my beats and I got my space, givin' in to them just ain't my fate."

Garret nodded, too stunned to try and reply.

In his teens he had exonerated the streets, and he had been warned he could get stuck there, but even his mother with her librarian self had said to him once "God is a call from the street" while she was reading her James Joyce. Back then he hadn't really thought about what that meant.

He bought a bottle of orange juice from Starbucks and handed it to the Real Change dude. This time the dude nodded approvingly without talking, opened the lid on the bottle, then gestured toward Garret in a toast and took a long sip.

When he got to the office the receptionist wasn't in yet. He turned on the lights in the office kitchen and started a pot of coffee. Faxes were coming in, but the only office that was lit up was in the back where a tech guy was working on the Y2K upgrade. Garret started on the spreadsheets for the CPA, which were basically boiler plate. The only real uncertainty was the value of the appraisal, which he would have any day now, but he was sure they were looking at a million at least.

"Hey, guy, how'd your trip go up on the Skagit?"

Garret looked up quickly. It was Larry, leaning against his doorway, coffee mug in hand.

"Outstanding! The place was beautiful. It's got a lot of big old trees and we saw a pair of eagles on the river. Ruthie from the Conservancy is a cool lady. The only downside is that the landowners have a jerk for a son-in-law, and he's their lawyer."

Larry raised an eyebrow at that so Garret explained the exchange he'd had with Dan, including the comment about the Caucasian Nations.

"Sounds like a nut case. Plus their having a relative as their lawyer might be a little close for comfort."

"I'm with ya on that one. You know, Larry, I try not to agonize over cases. It's not good for the soul. I try to maintain a certain level of detachment so that the thing works itself out by its own internal momentum, and I basically just help clients get to where they wanted to go from the beginning."

"I like that, man. Like a zen approach to banking."

"But this guy, he threw me off base and got me upset. I even offered to drop out of the case, which I've never done before."

"Heck no…"

"But the folks from the conservation group, they said they still want me on it."

"Hell yes. I mean, it's this guy's attitude problem, not yours."

"But I was thinking," Garret continued, "just so the family doesn't use this as an excuse to bail, I thought it might be more professional if I brought in another trust officer and I wondered if you'd be willing to jump in. Course we'd share the credit."

"If you think it'll help then I'm all for it. We'll double-team him. It's just a matter of making a few clean passes."

Garret chuckled. He knew Larry was something of a jock, played college football, and was a big fan of the Seahawks and the Sonics.

"We'll double team him and we won't take no for an answer!" Larry added.

"Thanks man. I appreciate it. You've got more history with folks out here, and I believe in learning from the locals. And you're a voracious closer!"

Larry laughed. "Let's just say I've had a good year. I love this business and trying to solve the puzzles that come along."

"Then it's a deal. I'll get us a meeting."

"Go get 'em Garret!"

As Larry left his office, Garret felt relieved. Being a Lone Ranger on a major deal that was leaning toward toxic would be no picnic.

At 10:00 a.m., Mark Bryant from the Setag Foundation arrived and Garret took him into a small conference room. Bryant was a youngish lawyer, probably about Garret's age. He was dressed in a three-piece suit and carried a large briefcase. As they sat down he glanced at the door which Garret immediately closed.

Bryant had a thin face and narrow shoulders and moved abruptly. "Well, Mr. Carter, I know we haven't given you much background. The foundation is extremely new. In fact, it hasn't really been staffed up yet. That's why they've called on me."

He opened his briefcase, pulled out a file and set it on the table. "How can I put this? The founders want to make a difference, and they have the funds to make a huge difference—in areas where philanthropy has barely existed in the past. They don't want to be part of some old boys' network, with the same tired old ideas." Bryant paused and looked Garret in the eye. He seemed to be waiting for Garret to say something.

"Of course not," Garret responded, not sure what the guy was getting at. "The bank can be a resource to you in finding links to the community in all sorts of sectors."

"I agree. But this could be one of the biggest foundations in the country if not the biggest. And in a society like this one, it takes real money to make real change."

"I wouldn't quarrel with that."

"The founders are concerned about world health, education, literacy, poverty, and an array of other local issues."

Garret nodded slowly, folding his hands together in front of him. "We've got some new tools in the works to help philanthropists establish better benchmarks. Tools that make the outcomes more quantifiable." Of course, until the tech guys got rid of the Y2K bugs, these tools would be on the back burner.

"Mr. Carter—Garret, if I may? How can I put this? The funds will be spread around to various financial institutions, locally and nationally. I know what the bank can do, but this conversation really isn't about choosing money managers." He paused, tapping his fingers lightly on the file he'd set down. "It's about values, about opportunities for people who haven't had any, about curing diseases, about educating people, about leveling out the playing field. This foundation is supposed to help change the world."

Bryant pulled back the sleeves of his jacket, unbuttoned his shirt cuffs, and rolled up his sleeves like he was getting ready to change a tire.

"We'd like to invite you to be on our advisory committee."

Garret began to cough, got up, and grabbed some water from the side table, managing to calm his throat. He realized he hadn't offered Bryant anything to drink.

"I'm sorry Mark, where are my manners? Would you like coffee or water?"

"No, no, I'm fine." Bryant waved his hand, motioning for Garret to relax. "I don't blame you for being a little surprised. We've been doing all these meetings in person, so that people would understand we're sincere about our recruiting. We're not just looking for the same old tired names—the people who appear on half the boards in town and rubber stamp everything so it's all status quo."

Bryant braced his elbows on the table and leaned forward earnestly. "No, we're looking for some new blood. It's hard to find people to serve in an advisory capacity who are willing to think outside the box, beyond any sort of personal allegiances. To look at real need locally and globally. Of course, the founders will be extremely involved and they'll make the final decisions."

Garret felt slightly flushed. "I have to tell you, I've served on a couple of non-profit boards, youth-oriented things, but those were places where I was already doing volunteer work. I've never advised a foundation before."

"Well, good." Bryant leaned back in his seat. "Because this isn't going to be like any other foundation advisory board. We assume the bank is paying you a relatively comfortable salary?"

Garret nodded. It was comfortable pay considering he was fairly new to the business. "Let's say I'm comfortable, but not complacent."

Bryant looked at him a little quizzically and then cracked a smile. "Committee members don't get paid, but we expect to provide you with some excellent networking opportunities. Generally, our meetings will be every other month, with a little prep work between. I'm sure you'll need time to think it over. So, what questions do you have?"

"Well, in terms of education, do you have any particular agenda?"

"I can tell you the founders are very concerned about Initiative 200—the initiative that outlawed affirmative action in public universities in this state. They feel we'll need to address some of the resulting setbacks."

"Right. I'm concerned about that, too. I-200 was one of the things about moving here that I considered a negative."

Garret took another sip of water, realizing that he had started to sweat. "So are you talking about some sort of mechanism to fund minority education?"

"Exactly," Bryant said, nodding. "Our plan is to design a national scholarship program. Of course it's up to you, but we thought you might be interested in working on a committee to get that moving." He seemed more relaxed now. "Our next meeting is two weeks from today, dinner at the Rainier Club. I'll call you next week and hopefully we can firm things up? Here's a list of who we have lined up so far." He flipped the file around so that it faced Garret and looked at this watch. "Say, I've got to run, but it's been great meeting you. Please give me a call if you have any questions—about anything at all." As he shook Garret's hand he added, "We believe that all people deserve a chance to lead a healthy and productive life."

"Is that sort of like a slogan for the foundation?"

"You got it. We're still hammering that out." He gave Garret a thumbs up as they walked out of the conference room.

After Bryant got on the elevator Garret felt like doing cartwheels down the hallway. He wanted to tell somebody the news—that Setag wanted *him*—and his first instinct was to dial up Jackie. That was how infused his life had been with her, but he shook his head.

Of course Sybil knew what was happening, so there was no point in telling her, either. He went to his office and dialed up his parents instead, and talked into their answering machine.

"Hey! I know you're probably at work, but you're not going to believe this! I just got recruited for the advisory board of the Setag Foundation! Sounds incredible. Call you later on!"

Ruthie stopped by The Rack at noon—a department store downtown—to get some cleats put on her favorite loafers. After she dropped them off in the repair department, she wandered down to the basement level to browse for a quick second and couldn't remember when she'd been in the store last. Her usual shopping routine was rummaging through second-hand stores.

Glancing along the racks, she was reminded of how many blouses and dresses were designed to resemble lingerie—a hint of lace here and there, a suggestive layer peeking out around the bodice. It wasn't her thing, but she was meeting Fioretti for dinner the next night at Wild Ginger and she wouldn't mind having *something* new to wear.

Of course, she thought, as she flipped through the racks looking for something a little more her style, if she were as gifted in one-upmanship as Fioretti and his crowd had been back in the day, her next move would be to call him an hour before the dinner and cancel. Maybe she should—it wasn't as if she had been pining over him since high school.

She noticed a bright green knit dress, fitted yet casual, which stood out from the boring grays and blacks that lined the rows. She pulled it out to take a better look. Of course, dressing up specially for Fioretti struck her as just a bit corny, but, just for old time's sake? She couldn't forget that he'd been seriously involved with Janet Dymond—after he'd dumped her, after the night of "the big R," of Rejection—so was it ego driving her? Or, heaven forbid, narcissism?

She put the green dress over her arm, located a bright green matching push-up bra, and brought them to the dressing rooms. As she fit her breasts into the bra, it occurred to her that she was now more well-endowed than she had been in high school, but it had been ages since she'd put on underwear that might be seen. She slipped on the dress. The tucks above the waist accentuated the roundness of her breasts, revealing just a little cleavage and a thin row of lace from the bra. Not a bad fit.

Honestly, she didn't know what she was doing. But, she thought, looking in the mirror at her figure, there was something intoxicating about remembering someone you knew when you were sixteen and he was sixteen, when you really had no clue what was happening in your body except for that simple feeling of electricity. She remembered a time, leaving a movie theater, her fingertips lightly touching the bare skin of his back under his shirt ... spontaneous and sensual.

But that electricity wasn't enough to make her ignore the memory of disappointment she'd felt, disappointment that had become almost existential, after The Big R. She'd been devastated. It came back in flashes: he asked her for a friend's phone number and took up with her, which made it worse. She'd wondered how he could shift his focus so quickly when all she'd been doing really was testing him, looking for the right time and the right place, something better than the back of some guy's grungy van. She'd started writing poetry, and when her mother gave her a small Italian dictionary so that she might learn a few phrases to try on him, she burst into tears.

When her existential angst took her to the student union soon after The Big R, she ran into a guy named Yanachek, who was loosely connected with Fioretti's crowd and something of a poet. Ruthie dribbled out the events of the previous few weeks—that Fioretti had stopped seeing her because she wouldn't sleep with him—and Yanachek's response surprised her.

"Well, more power to you," he said. "That's what he deserves!"

She looked vacantly at him, stirring sugar into her black coffee.

"Don't you see?" he explained. "You've won a contest of wills against the great Cameron Fioretti! You deserve a medal!"

If it was a victory, it was bittersweet, and Yanachek's eyes had looked glassy; she wondered if he too had a crush on Fioretti.

"Honey, you're too good for Cameron Fioretti. Don't you understand that?" he said, toasting her.

She thought he was putting her on.

Since then, Fioretti had become a successful documentary filmmaker, and he'd just finished a new project on political asylum for public television which had gotten a lot of publicity. Of course, she had moved on. After high school she'd gotten involved with a guy from the U.W. in a relationship that had a beginning, a middle, and an end. But she never thought about that guy the way she thought about Fioretti.

And now? She was embarrassed even to admit to herself how she felt now—the involuntary tensing of her thighs, the warming and tightening of her crotch. It was her biology talking. This was nothing you could fake, nothing you could learn, nothing you could cultivate.

She looked in the mirror again and wondered who it was in the universe who might appreciate her raw natural vitality. Fioretti? Well, that was a question. Who could say how many women he had loved, or at least tried to conquer, since she'd seen him last?

And why, she thought shaking her head and smoothing the fabric of the dress over her waist, why the hell was she—at the age of almost thirty—allowing herself to revisit all of this again?

Still... the dress wasn't a bad fit. She smiled. It'd be a shame to waste it. For old time's sake, she thought. She rarely wore eye make-up, but decided some green eye shadow would look cool with the dress, and after she slipped back into her own clothes she went searching for some.

Garret walked into the venue on time and found Vance already there, holding down a table with a young woman.

"Nadine, this dude actually lives within walking distance of Jazz Alley and he's only lived here a week," Vance said as he walked up. "Garret, this is my fiancée Nadine. Nadine, meet my good buddy Garret."

"Garret, we saved you the best seat in the house," she said, flashing a smile. "Shoot, Vance told me you were smart but he didn't mention handsome."

Garret laughed as he sat down. "Oh hey, he wanted to keep the best a surprise, Nadine. It's great to finally meet you. Now I see why my buddy didn't come back home much."

"Yup, it's just me and computers keeping his life full. Just so long as he doesn't get us mixed up." She pecked Vance on the cheek.

"So—how's it goin' big guy?" Vance asked, giving him some skin. "How was the first week?"

"Whew—feelin' kinda chewed up. Like they might be getting ready to spit me out!"

"They should be lettin' you coast the first couple weeks, man."

"I know. I tell ya, feels like they've been storin' stuff up for me. My boss gave me a load of her clients, this co-worker is looking for somebody to cover his butt on a deal that went south, a rich lady came on to me over at Pacific Place, and a redneck client tried to initiate a debate about the Caucasian Nations."

Nadine and Vance both laughed, especially on the last comment.

"Goddamn, puttin' you to the test already! Nadine, I told you he'd be a big fish in no time."

Garret held out his hands and shook his head. "Man, they got more work than people and nobody ready to take any heat—

or dumb enough to. You know what I'm saying… So Nadine, how's the student teaching going?"

"I see Vance has been filling you in." She smiled over at him. "Busy as ever. Right now I'm doing eleventh grade language arts at Garfield High School. It's hard work, but I'm lucky to have a black teacher as my supervisor. He seems to have a lot of integrity. I never met anybody who was so literary but can still switch into Ebonics gears just like snapping your fingers. You would not believe! That's how he connects with lots of the kids and parents."

"Isn't Garfield supposed to be one of the best high schools in the city?"

"Sure, but it's got some problems just like anyplace."

"Well, Nadine is a natural," Vance told him. "She knows how to talk to kids. She's got other experiences to share, other things she's done besides teaching."

"So Garret, have you heard Redman before?" she asked him.

"Not in person. Just collected a lot of his CDs. I'm psyched."

"Nadine, Garret used to be a boss sax player in high school—and in college."

Nadine raised her eyebrows at Garret and handed him the breadbasket. "How about now? Do you still play?"

"Not much. It's kind of a crime." He took some bread and poured a little olive oil onto his bread plate.

Nadine nodded. "Like Vance with his bass. Now that you two have your careers on track, you oughta get together and play some."

"Hey, I'm way out of practice," Vance told her.

They ordered some Italian food and Vance suggested a bottle of Montepulciano.

"Sounds good to me," Garret told him. "Kickin' back with an old buddy and his hope-to-die." Charlie Parker was wailing through the sound system. So far he liked this place.

"You know," he said, settling into his seat, "a really bizarre thing did go down this week. A guy came into the office, a lawyer, and started recruiting me for the advisory board of the Setag Foundation."

"You puttin' me on, man?"

"No, I'm serious. They need people to get some of their grantmaking programs started."

"I told you, man. Nadine, I've been tryin' to get Garret out here for years. Shoot, I don't know your business, but that sounds like some kind of pinnacle to me! In the first week, no less!"

"Congratulations!" Nadine added.

"Course, you never know what brand of tokenism may be operating," Garret said, hedging a bit. "But the lawyer claimed they want to invest some major money into scholarships for minority students."

"Well, if the money is going to be put to positive uses, then hey, make your voice heard, know what I'm sayin'?" she said.

After the wine arrived, Vance lifted his glass. "Here's to my long lost buddy—my Chicago brother makin' the scene out west and already creating a serious impression!"

"And to Vance," Garret said, joining in. "The primo software engineer, scoring stock options and hittin' the big time, and to his fiancée Nadine!"

"I'll drink to that," Vance said as they toasted, "but you gotta remember. Out here, writing code is as everyday as riding a bicycle."

"Actually, Vance is working on a software package to help kids learn world history. So we're both dealing with the high school curriculum. Isn't that cool?" Nadine said after setting her glass back down.

"Awesome!"

"So, Vance told me about your girl Jackie. I was sorry to hear about that," Nadine added.

"Well, honey, do you need to bring it up?" Vance asked her.

"No, no, it's cool, man. I'm cool with it." Garret shifted in his seat. "I mean, it's not like she deliberately set out to hurt me. I went through all the usual stuff—you know, blaming the guy she's engaged to, all that. I mean, how is some white dude from Grosse Point, Michigan going to understand Jackie, know what I'm sayin'? I had this feeling of protection that set in—like is he going to misuse her, see? But he didn't force her to fall for him either. "

"No, but I can't really blame you ..." Vance said slowly.

"He's a doctor and all, and I visualized this scene where he burns her out. I've had plenty of macho feelings, like how I should have bought her an engagement ring when she got ready to move to Michigan, for instance, to sort of lock in our thing, but—" He noticed Nadine had a pretty fancy looking rock on her ring finger. "But it's her life. I finally realized I couldn't bribe her, and I certainly couldn't control her."

"Well, you know, Garret," Nadine said, "I worked in a hospital for awhile as a patient care coordinator. It's a hierarchical world—with doctors at the top, of course. It takes a lot of discipline to live in that universe and not completely buy into it. In that cosmology, everybody's looking for endorsement from the MDs. Any young woman could be very vulnerable to that."

"So, you're saying Jackie hit the jackpot," Vance said. "By marrying a doctor."

The words stung, but Garret knew what his buddy meant. "Well I guess that's right," he said. "She's going to be a positive force, whoever she's with, 'cause that's the kind of person she is. She's a natural healer."

Of course, Garret knew it hadn't just been about a ring. Jackie wasn't that shallow. But his inherent passivity in their relationship still plagued him. Lifting his wine glass to take a sip, he wondered if the men on his father's side carried a certain fatalism that spread to the way they treated women—or rather, didn't treat them, waiting for *them* to send the right signals instead. Still, what was so right about a take-charge MD who wanted to be treated like he could do no wrong? How confident does he act when one of his patients dies? But Garret hadn't actually met the dude.

The food arrived. His favorite Italian dish, cannelloni. With one ear on Vance and Nadine's conversation, he wondered if he would ever lose the bittersweet taste left by Jackie, or, more honestly, the way they'd been together—the taste left by perfect hindsight of what he might have done. The if-onlys… If only he could have hustled hard to try and get a job in Ann Arbor and close in on the relationship. Although Garret's rational mind said it was time to, he hadn't completely let go. That was why moving to Seattle made sense. He'd been coaching himself to move on, but part of him was still back there with her, back there in the space that was theirs and theirs alone.

"Hey, there's the drummer setting up!" Nadine said, interrupting his thoughts.

The bass player arrived next and then Joshua Redman was announced. He counted off a tune almost immediately after walking on stage, as if there weren't even seconds to lose. A Dexter Gordon tune, which they took at a fast tempo.

Redman's style was clipped and crisp; he was strict with his tempo, but he still gave the drummer the edge to set the pace. The band was up. Vance seemed to be transfixed, and Garret noted that all the musicians were young—late twenties, early thirties—and all intense players. Redman's density and range reminded Garret of Coltrane, a comparison that was rare. He was a young lion of jazz, who'd dropped out of law school to pursue the music.

As the tune ended there was a brief moment of tense silence, of total quiet. No one in the room even budged, and then suddenly everyone broke out into loud applause. Redman turned to the mike to say something but then changed his mind.

Garret heard him whisper to the band, ever so quietly, "Giant Steps," and they were off and running again, Redman still clearly in charge as they played it up-tempo. Then, very gradually, as Redman soloed, the tune expanded beyond its own boundaries, leaving open possibilities—variations you could imagine if you stretched—and then Redman executed those and others so intricately that the tune re-defined itself.

All the players seemed to be vulnerable to what felt like spontaneous changes. In one section, Redman dropped out and the bass player McBride introduced an alternate set of runs that evolved from the original changes, then McBride started comping and Redman somehow referred to the new set of changes, dissecting them into their most basic, crucial elements. It was a tribute to abstraction, leading into a drum solo that captured the audience so intensely that Garret could feel the people around him holding their breath, encouraging the young drummer Brian Blade to subdivide to his heart's content. The tension was incredible until, finally, Redman and McBride joined back in on the head of the tune, triggering an applause that was huge—maybe as much a release of tension as it was the audience's realization of their vulnerability. The audience clapped and shouted and yet Redman appeared humbled, overwhelmed by the unlimited possibilities of this large music. He thought Redman almost looked amazed at finding himself in the middle of it.

It would be a good night.

Chapter Five

†

Monday morning, on his way into work, Garret saw the brother with the short locks stationed in front of the building holding a stack of newspapers.

"If you're not lame, you'll read Real Change," he said.

Garret had only skimmed his first copy but he discovered the paper was created to benefit homeless people.

The guy went on, "It won't give you wealth or give you fame, but expand your mind and pave the way, 'cause sharin' the wealth is the name of the game."

Garret handed him a dollar, took a copy of the paper, and almost started to rhyme something, but it wasn't happening. Some other dude came along with a two-dollar bill and Garret nodded at the brother and went inside.

He went up to Larry's office to see if he wanted to hook up at noon and check out the car auction place but nobody was around. Larry had been the one to tell him this auction garage in Wallingford was a low-pressure way to buy a car using silent bids. The office felt strangely quiet. As he walked back toward his office, Sybil came towards him from further down the hall.

"Garret, may I see you for a minute?" she asked, her voice sounding more strained than usual.

"Sure," he said with more certainty than he felt, and they headed toward his office.

Shutting his door she said, "I wanted to tell you first, because I know you've got some pending business with Larry. We've had to let him go."

"Larry?" Garret was stunned, and for a moment he thought maybe he didn't hear her right.

"I'm afraid so. He was a big producer, but … It's hard to explain. There were some situations recently, where he just didn't complete the paperwork we needed on delicate types of cases."

He thought it felt like she was holding something back, but he couldn't tell what. "Like the Nielsen case?"

"Well yes, for one," she said, shifting her weight and glancing towards the window. "There were others, too, although we managed to more or less salvage most of those. But Mrs. Nielsen pulled more than ten million dollars out of the bank, and honestly, we're lucky she didn't sue. We'd warned Larry before about things like this—about following through on the trust memos and documenting his client contacts. We can't afford to have important client information stored exclusively in one person's head."

She spread her hands out in front of her and shook her head, as if to show Garret how patient she'd been with Larry, as if she had tried to help him succeed and he was the one who failed. But it still didn't feel right.

"All information, it's the property of the bank, and it needs to be stored in our data base. As you know," she said and looked at him for a response.

"Well, I honestly don't know the full history, but I have to tell you… I like Larry. Seems to me, his positive energy can help make a deal happen. He can see the big picture, set things in motion, and let the deal sail through like a clean pass across a basketball floor."

Garret suddenly had the sinking feeling that Larry fit into this scene way better than he did. Larry could spar with the guys in the elevator who talked about elephant hunting, about zinging that big account that would ace their careers. Larry loved it, but for Garret this work was just the least evil thing he could think of to do as a lawyer. And if Larry was expendable, where did that leave him?

"That's why I was counting on him in this McGowan case," Garret said, trying not to sound worked up.

"I'm sorry Garret. I don't blame you for being upset. It was a tough choice."

She looked away as if she had been about to reveal too much. Maybe Larry had been right when he'd hinted that one of them might have to go.

Sybil cleared her throat, and when she spoke again her voice returned to normal. "What I wanted to say was that I admire you for doing the right thing—for putting together a team to save the McGowan case. Is there anyone else who could partner with you on this one?"

"I don't know. As you've probably heard, the donor's son-in-law seems to have a lot of hostility. Nancy has the expertise, but this guy is probably sexist, too. Looks to me like Peter has the backbone, but I'm afraid he's just a little green. I don't want to give this guy an excuse to throw a boomerang over the whole deal."

"People don't realize how psychological this business is." Sybil smiled and started to move towards his door to leave. "Go ahead and bring in a consultant if you need to. Al Crawford has helped us out before."

Garret nodded and wrote the guy's name down. He doubted this Crawford guy would have the same skin in the game as Larry.

He called the car auction place and found out he had the highest bid on a '95 Honda Accord. He just didn't get this Larry thing. Here he was, the one dude in the office Garret could actually relate to, and he got axed. If Cybil let the biggest producer go, then she had no permanent loyalties. Sure, she may be picking Garret for some plum assignments right now but that could change. Even her name had a fickle quality to it.

Maybe his father had been right. On the way to the airport, Garret had talked about the new job and about how Seattle was known as a progressive city and even had a black mayor. "Well I'm not sure what you can conclude from that," his father had said. "Working on the south side of Chicago, you weren't in a minority. You had folks who knew you. People you went to high school with and played with in Little League became your customers. Most of your friends didn't resent you working that gig. They'd seen you under cars enough times holding a wrench and hot-rodding around on week-ends too much to hold it against you for getting ahead. But in Seattle, who knows? If you want to succeed in a place like Seattle, you'll have to be twice as good."

He'd barely paid attention when his father had said it, but now he was beginning to think he had a point.

In the afternoon Garret had a trustee errand to deliver a check from a small foundation to a middle school that served homeless children. The school was up Jackson Street next to a bakery, in a long two-story building that looked as old as the middle school he had gone to back in Chicago. As he parked and got out of the bank car the scent of baking bread was oddly comforting.

The back of the building looked almost deserted. When he walked around to the front door he saw "NoMorePrisons.net" scrawled in lettering so familiar he could have sworn it was done by the same hand as the tags he'd seen on the sidewalks of Chicago.

As he opened the front door, he was suddenly hit with the din of yelling children, a chaotic maze of bodies in motion. Could his own school have been this crazy and loud and he had somehow adjusted to it?

He thought Seattle's public schools were supposed to be good, but looking around, he couldn't help but notice that this place looked as old, out of repair, and crowded as the old schools on the South Side. Weaving through the packed hall, he found his way to the office and asked the secretary for the teacher who was in charge of the assembly.

The office even smelled the same as his middle school—the dusty paper smell, some overly sweet cologne, and the inevitable school lunchroom smell not far off. In middle school he'd been labeled a high achiever—academics, music, sports, even karate. He'd done everything his parents had asked and it wasn't until later, in high school, that he'd started to question it all. In his senior yearbook, where others were labeled with things like "Most Likely to Succeed," a photo showed him with his hair long, his jeans sagging, holding a video game with the caption "Garret Carter - Most Changed" under it.

Suddenly, a tall slender woman with long grayish hair that frizzed out to the sides rushed through the door and, somewhat out of breath, introduced herself as Sandy Sheridan. Garret shook her hand as she explained that there would be an assembly starting any minute and that he would be introduced after the jazz band's performance.

The band was already playing when he followed her into an auditorium brimming with students. The players sounded more like adults than kids—a tight sound, for sure. The director was a slim African American guy with thick glasses who had incredible command of the group. Sandy motioned toward a couple of seats on the bleachers near the front.

"These guys are great," he said to Sandy, leaning towards her so that she could hear him over the band and the shouts of students.

She smiled a frazzled smile and pointed to a group of kids along the right of the stage. "Those kids take an art class after school and get a hot meal—thanks to your foundation. Excuse me, Garret, I have to get my other group ready back stage."

He relaxed into his seat as the band played "Satin Doll," with a couple kids playing the head as a trumpet feature.

He had played in the jazz band in middle school and practiced hard. Listening to these kids, he couldn't help but feel a twinge of nostalgia for the life he'd led when he was their age, when his biggest conflict was being double booked because he had a basketball game at the same time he was supposed to play alto clarinet in some competition.

In high school he got into the best high school jazz band in the city on saxophone. He'd considered majoring in music and his father had encouraged it, saying he had the chops. But by his junior year in high school, he'd lost the discipline he'd developed and his solos were becoming more original than polished.

He'd started smoking weed, even at school sometimes, and hanging out with older dudes who had dropped out of school. At that point, his focus on music shifted and he acquired a desire to make money on his own, to not be as limited as his parents were, to try and find some way to make a living without struggling like the guys he knew who played jazz or taught music. Those guys always seemed to be broke. His dad had said that money wasn't everything but Garret wouldn't listen.

Listening to the kids in front of him, playing their hearts out on "Take the A Train," reminded him he hadn't really begun to unravel his feelings about that period of his life until he got to college and met Jackie.

Jackie was in the Get Over It school before it became the thing. When he'd complained that his parents were too asocial, she'd say he was lucky they were still alive and well.

"Your parents had to be incredibly loyal just to stay together," she'd said. "Besides. Everybody has beef about their parents, or their upbringing, or their supposedly short stick."

When he said some professor had it in for him, she told him to stop doing his work under the wire and start getting organized. She said he was an auditory learner, so when he was studying for tests he should read the material into a tape recorder and listen to it over and over. It worked, and got him through the LSATs and through law school. She wasn't into enabling him; she was more about solutions.

Jackie had said that there was only one thing harder for people than recovering from what their parents had done to them, and that was becoming parents themselves. But how had she known that at her tender age? He knew she'd learned a lot from her patients during her psychology internship at the clinic. She said the work was about helping to relieve their burden by taking some of the weight, and she had an amazing ability that was deceptively simple: she knew how to listen. It was uncanny and powerful to have someone devote their full attention the way she did—to listen and be totally present. He had taken it for granted but, in hindsight, that was one of the things he missed the most.

He had started to figure her out, too. He realized that when she came home from working at the hospital and jumped in the shower, she was through being a problem-solver. She just wanted to relax. She'd have an idea for some new recipe, or she'd show up with a comedy video. A few times she brought home crossword puzzles, which she was incredibly good at. She was a master at switching gears and not dwelling on her day. She even wrote a food list, claiming it was for her nieces and nephews, but he was pretty sure it had been mainly for him: "The Super Cheap and Easy Food List for Young Men and Other Folks." He actually did start using it, because it was cheap and easy and, because it was written by Jackie, it was much healthier than buying burgers and pizza. *Number one: Toss a Salad,* it said. *Grab some lettuce and any veggies you have in the fridge. Throw in some grated cheese and a hard-boiled egg for protein.*

When the jazz band finished, the principal announced they had won first place at a jazz contest—named after Lionel Hampton—in Moscow, Idaho. Then a group of kids performed a skit about nuclear disarmament, with Sandy Sheridan coaching on the side. Even though the topic was serious, there was a lilt to their voices, a rhythm that was familiar, like the sounds of kids in the neighborhood, auditory totems from his childhood etched in the recesses of his memory. He started to nod off but was suddenly jolted awake by a loud screech from the sound system.

Sandy grabbed the mike, as if this were her cue to introduce the group of student artists lining the opposite wall. The kids paraded onto stage carrying paintings and sculpture in all shapes and sizes. Sandy called Garret onto the stage to present the foundation check, and he managed to improvise a few words into the mike. After a loud applause, the principal made some announcements, the students got up, and the chaos started again.

When he got back to the office he found a package on his desk. The package contained a photo of a pair of eagles from the day he and Ruthie were on the McGowan property—a beautiful blow-up, of light penetrating the clouds above the trees, a patch of mist in front, and the eagles in focus above the dark water—in a frame with a note from Ruthie saying "Remember the eagles." She obviously knew what she was doing with a camera.

On Friday, after a long staff meeting, Garret had a voice mail from Ruthie asking him if the CPA had called back. He checked through the rest of his messages to see. He hadn't.

Damn, Garret thought. Talking to CPAs was his specialty—enough so that he might have been able to lock in this deal without Larry, just by dealing with the CPA directly and not focusing on Dan's creepy attitude. While other lawyers got hung up talking about legal precedents and on-the-other-hands, Garret got to the bottom line, focusing on things like income and tax benefits.

He called Ruthie back to let her know it looked like Dan and the CPA weren't playing ball. She asked if he'd gotten a fax from Dan. He hadn't.

"It says it was sent to both of us, that Arnie has taken a turn for the worse, and not to contact him or Mrs. McGowan right now."

"Crap. He's tying our hands. With instructions like that, we're going to have to cool it or it makes your organization look bad."

"That's what I was afraid of. I've never felt so excluded before. Ejected from something I thought was important and urgent. Besides... My boss really wants us to make this happen. It's a high priority."

"I get that. Unfortunately, we don't have a green light to do much of anything here unless the CPA calls back. That looks like our only window. You don't want to be sued for undue influence later on." He hated sounding lawyer-ish and realized he should have explained it some other way. Then she said she had another call and after they hung up, he wished he had invited her to lunch or found some reason to get together. But his job was to find a solution, not just get together so they could both cry in their beers.

His stomach growled and he realized it was 1:00. He went down to the food court, in a lower level of the office building, where some of the lines were still long.

A guy wearing a court jester cap with the bells hanging off of several tassels was handing out leaflets near the escalator. As Garret got closer, he recognized him.

"Larry! What's up man? Been wondering about you!"

"Hey man! It's Good-Grief-dot-com, check it out," he said, handing Garret a bright red flyer, the same color as his court jester hat. A lot of folks were picking up his flyers.

"You eating down here, man?" Larry asked as Garret glanced down at the flyer. "I'll join you when this crowd thins out."

"Sure thing! How 'bout some chicken teriyaki?" Larry gave him a thumbs up.

Garret filled up a tray and found a table close to the escalators. Larry's flyer explained that GoodGrief.com offered stock trades and investment news for private investors, plus tax tips, retirement planning, house buying, and the Northwest stock special. It seemed like Larry was finding a niche for himself, though Garret wasn't sure how he could get paid just by launching a website.

"Well, I'm all out of flyers," Larry said as he walked up a few minutes later. "Can you believe it? In one hour, I've carried out my marketing plan for whole the day! Course I know a lot of people in this building, so I'm sure as heck not intimidated by the idea of running into Sybil or one of her young lieutenants. Say, this lunch looks great. Thanks." He reached into his pocket for some cash, but Garret waved him off.

"This one's on me. So, man! It sure didn't take you long to get this off the ground."

"No. And I'm starting to get hits on the site, too. I've had an idea for quite awhile to do some kind of website for folks who want to do their own investing. Look at all the clients out there making good money in the stock market. You notice most of our rich clients at the bank? They were rich before they came to our trust department. And as far as brokers' commissions go, well, they're burnt out. That's why my web site could be catching on."

He was talking fast and chewing fast. Seemed like the same old Larry, confident as ever.

"Course, I can offer my services as an advisor, but it's not just me," he said, adding soy sauce to his chicken. "My site has links to all this free info, where regular folks can tap into experts. The sky's the limit! Course I want to have a Northwest focus since there are already sites like this. In my next edition there's a special on saving for your kid's college education and creating a foundation. There's some lifestyle tips, too, like my wife's personal favorite—how to eat right for your blood type. Bottom line is I want to help people get a handle on market trends. I'm not just talking fly-by-night."

"Oh, clearly… I mean, with that hat and all …" Garret raised an eyebrow and Larry chuckled. "So what are some of the major market trends?"

"Well, I tell ya," he said, taking another bite. "There are some self-fulfilling prophecies out there for sure. Those people ignoring fundamentals completely, well, they may do okay for awhile, you know, short term, but they're going to have to know when to pull out. People are into some of the smaller start-ups, but you have to take your chances there." He paused for a minute to chew.

"But we're still just beginning on the Internet wave, actually. We may only be a quarter of the way through it. Even the investment department at the bank will admit that. You can't go wrong investing in Internet infrastructure. People are recommending phone companies linked to the Internet, for instance, or business-to-business stuff on the Web."

"Sounds smart to me. Course I haven't had the time or the money to put into the stock market yet. I just picked the mutual funds in the retirement package that are most heavily invested in tech stuff, and put in almost the maximum allowed."

"Good move."

"So, how'd you come up with a name like GoodGrief.com?"

"Well, it was a strange thing. Last Friday—" Larry shook his head. "God, I can't believe it was only a week ago. Anyway, I'm getting ready to go home, right? And Sybil calls me into her office, shuts the door, and drops the bomb on me."

"Oh just like that, huh?"

"Yeah, right. Just like that. She says something generic, like 'we're going to have to let you go.' So I try and pin her down. I say, 'I think I have a right to know why, since I'm the biggest producer in the department.' I was curious to see if she would mention the Nielsen case, since she actually had some liability on that one, but she didn't. She was vague and said we didn't see eye-to-eye. She mentioned case documentation in general. Well, I was pissed."

Garret nodded, remembering the conversation in the lunchroom about that case.

"She wasn't leveling with me, so I didn't want to talk to her. I start thinking lawsuits and all that, but I keep cool, go into my office and start packing my stuff up. And then she walks in there and asks me if I need extra time to pack. But what she's really asking is when am I going to turn in my keys. I'm just so damn sick of people who can't be straight with me." He slapped the table for emphasis.

"So I finally get out of there, and of course I'm fuming all the way home. Get stuck on the bridge at the worst possible time, and I'm trying to decide how to break it to Delores, my wife. I mean, I know she's going to be stressed, right? Because she cut her hours way back so she could volunteer at our kid's school. But, just idling along on that bridge, I sort of talk myself out of being angry. I table it. Like, I figure I'll talk to an employment lawyer. I'll investigate to see if there's a legal angle to pursue, so that if somebody needs to be the bad cop, let the lawyer do it and save me the ulcer."

Larry leaned forward, his voice calming down. "You know, either I take her to court or I get Sybil to admit that there never was a Nielsen trust memo and she is ultimately responsible for that, so as far as the firing went, it was her or me. So maybe there's a cash settlement. But the real issue," Larry paused for emphasis, "the real issue is my recovery. So I'm just sitting there on the bridge, and I start thinking about other things I could do, and I've already got the skeleton of the website. Just need to beef it up. Course, I didn't have a name for it yet. But I call my wife from the car and ask her out to dinner and she's upbeat about that, says the kids have plans and she's in the mood to go out.

"So by the time I let the news out, well, I'm opening a wine bottle in the restaurant, and I kind of break it to her gently. She knows the banking business is dog-eat-dog, so I tell her what happened, expecting some kind of reaction, you know? But before she says anything, she takes a deep breath, and sort of sympathetically, she says, 'Good grief.'"

"So that's how you got the name."

"Yeah. It kinda makes sense, salesman that I am—taking the situation and turning it into something positive. It's grief, sure, but I look for a way to make it good. Besides, the site was available." Larry smiled.

"Well, man, alright. Here's to you, Larry!" Garret raised his paper cup. "You got a lot of heart! Although," he said as the two of them toasted, "it may take me a little while to get used to you in that hat..."

Larry shook his head and the bells of his cap jingled.

"The foundation was created because the benefactors want change, not status quo. And it's foundations—more than governments, more than corporations—that have been the catalysts for the most progressive changes in this country."

It was Paul Setag, Senior speaking, the father of the foundation's main benefactor.

"It happened with Carnegie. It happened with Rockefeller. It happened with Ford in the twentieth century. And now, thanks to the revolution in information technology, as we approach the end of the century, it's about to happen with Setag in the twenty-first."

He went on to outline how the foundation had started by sending people to libraries of the rural south, encouraging them to use computers—the great equalizer. And how it was expanding to fund health organizations all over the world, helping to inoculate the world's children. He said he would introduce the main speaker after dinner.

"Well, it takes more than computers to educate folks," said Wayne, the fellow next to Garret at the foundation dinner. "It's no panacea," he added in a mild southern accent.

Garret didn't expect to hear that from the CEO of a high tech company. He'd seen Wayne's name on the lists of several non-profit boards in town. According to Ruthie, his company had made major donations to conservation groups.

"It's going to take awhile for the foundation to establish its priorities," said Cliff, the guy on Garret's right, an African American brother who was an admissions officer at the U.W. "If they're serious, the foundation could fill in where I-200 tied our hands."

Several people at the table agreed, including Mark Bryant, the recruiter who was sitting across from Garret, and Ruby, the Hispanic woman sitting next to Cliff, who worked at Evergreen State College.

"The question is, do you want to spread wide or do you want to go deep?" Ruby asked.

"Well, I think you gotta try and do both," Cliff answered, weighing his words. "The only way to make it worth doing is to have a serious impact on a student, so he or she can stay in school. There are plenty of one thousand dollar scholarships out there."

Clearly everyone at his table was on the scholarship committee. The woman sitting next to Wayne, an older white woman who worked at a local community foundation, said they needed to establish a minimum GPA. As the waiter offered them more wine, Garret noticed Madeleine Knight sitting at another table across the room.

"We actually have more infrastructure in this state for funding endangered species than we do taking care of people who are at risk," said Cliff.

"I hadn't thought of it quite that way," said Wayne mildly. "I mean, the main reason I came out here and stayed is I like being in the mountains, and saving wilderness seems really important. But I agree about this state and the need for improving education. We're behind a lot of other states in the aid department. Take Georgia, with their Hope Scholarships—they're funded by the state lottery. I never understood why we had to link tree cutting with schools."

"For real. The Setag Foundation is looking at some major K-12 initiatives," Ruby told him. "We're considering hiring a principal from one of the local school districts to start the project." Mark nodded.

The waiters brought plates of grilled salmon and vegetables.

"So Garret, Ruth over at the Conservancy said you're involved with playing jazz," Wayne said.

"Well, I used to play a lot," Garret told him. "Mainly saxophone."

"It's the darnest thing. My daughter is only nine and she wants to take up the saxophone. I got her a guitar, but it didn't really grab her. When she asked the teacher about sax, he told her she should start with clarinet first."

"Yup, music teachers usually say that. That's what I did in fourth grade. I'd say go ahead and start with clarinet, but have her remind the teacher every so often she wants to switch. As long as she works hard on her embouchure, he might let her switch after a year or so."

"Thanks for the tip. I'm just trying to keep up with her."

Garret smiled. He wasn't used to hearing a southern drawl come from a guy who wasn't a cracker.

He looked up at the largest crystal chandelier he had ever seen in his life. This place was definitely old guard: polished old wood the color of dark walnut, crystal everywhere, and wide staircases with portraits in heavy frames of famous Native Americans on the walls. He doubted many of their descendants had set foot in the place.

"How 'bout this wild salmon, huh man?" Cliff asked.

"It's gotta be the best I ever tasted," Garret told him. It really was delicious.

"The main chef here is supposed to be a brother from the Caribbean with lots of skills. You know, you just can't predict where folks are gonna show up."

Garret nodded. "I'm tellin' ya. I've been thinking along those lines since I moved out here. Seems like I see some people who look like they're striving big time, and I have to catch myself, expecting them to act phony. This one dude I work with has this disarming way of pretty much letting it all hang out. Course he just got laid off, so he doesn't have much to lose."

"I s'pose people here seem a little more casual than back East?"

"They definitely seem more laid back. So what about you, man? Are you a local?"

"Born and raised. My grandmother's still living over there in the C.D.—the Central District. And both of my folks, too. Me and my brothers, we're what you could call local agitators. Actually, my older brother Ernie was one of the first Black Panthers in Seattle, helped organize the children's free breakfast program all through the seventies, into the eighties. I have to give him a lot of credit, he's an activist from the word go. He's fourteen years older, so I was pretty young when he got started, but I'll never forget him standing on the street corners day after day, in all kinds of weather, holdin' out a can asking for change for the children's free breakfast program. He got a lot of support in the U. District, I remember that."

"So what's he up to now?"

"He's the same old Ernie. Now he's working on prison reform, and also trying to get funding for more GED programs—on television, in prisons, community colleges, wherever. I don't wanna brag—it's not about that. It's just—he's one of the few left from the Panther days who hasn't either sold out into some form of local politics or gotten killed, or just sort of gone off the deep end. Know what I'm sayin'?"

"Yeah, man." Garret nodded. "And how 'bout you? How long have you been working in the admissions office?"

"It's only been three years. But it's great—there's been something unique about seeing kids come through who I've known from way back when I was a teacher at John Muir Elementary School. Course, since I-200 passed, we're not the Office of Minority Affairs anymore. To pretend that it didn't impact minority enrollment is bull."

"Well, you deserve a lot of credit for stickin' it out in your community and helping some kids get up through the educational system."

The waiters brought in dessert and coffee. Setag got back on stage to introduce the main speaker, Colleen Jackson, who was one of the first black women in the state legislature and was now working on another advanced degree.

Colleen told them that her topic was extraordinary people, like some local activists, and the role that education played in their lives. Then she focused on Martin Luther King. "But in the case of I-200, we were not vigilant. Ward Connerly stole King's words and took them out of context," she said from the podium, and Garret could hear murmurs from the room.

"Amen," Cliff muttered beside him.

"We forget that King said we could all join hands together, in the words of the old Black spiritual, and sing: Free at last, free at last, thank God almighty, we're free at last. In the words of the old black spiritual, ladies and gentlemen, in the words of a long-standing African American tradition, born out of *our* experience. He was asking people of all races to learn from us, to spend some time with *our* culture, *our* history."

Her voice had a resonance that really held peoples' attention, and Garret thought she sounded sincere. The whole room was quiet.

"He wasn't saying we have to give up our culture in order to live in this society. He was saying our culture is powerful and beautiful and contagious." She took a sip of water.

"The media has focused so much on King's nonviolence. We have forgotten how intensely radical civil disobedience can be. King and Rosa Parks paved the way, to sit where we want to sit and march where we want to march. Not only Civil Rights, but the peace movement, the women's movement, labor rights, poor peoples' campaigns, even the right to keep Mother Earth alive."

"Amen, sister," said Cliff loudly, and then more quietly to Garret, "She may be mainstream, but she's got something to say. There's a lotta people out there tried to de-radicalize King."

Slowly, people in the room started clapping and standing up. As Cliff and Garret stood, the others at their table followed. Setag, Senior thanked Ms. Jackson and made some closing remarks, and Mark Bryant handed out a large packet to everyone at the table.

As people shook hands around the table, it seemed to Garret that most of the attention was directed toward Cliff and himself. He wouldn't stoop to calling it white guilt, but perhaps some form of Afrocentrism was unleashed by the speech. Whatever caused it, Cliff was not about to lose out on the opportunity.

"Look," he said, "I'm going to level with you folks here on this committee. I believe that foundations can make a difference, even help get a new project off the ground that would never make it otherwise. And this one is about fighting diseases, and about literacy and educating poor folks. And I buy that, don't get me wrong. But philanthropy is no substitute for social justice, and no committee is going to make me pretend it is."

Garret started to say that he agreed, but the woman next to Wayne interrupted, muttering her goodbyes as she collected her purse and left.

"It ain't no substitute, Cliff. I agree with you," Wayne said.

With that drawl of his, Wayne probably used words like "ain't" even around white folks, Garret thought.

"Foundations have to be a voice for change, or they don't deserve their tax-favored status. Compared to governments or corporations, they're the most progressive voice we've got."

"In my book, grass roots organizations are the ones coming up with real solutions. But they hardly get noticed for funding," Cliff told him.

"How 'bout we continue this conversation?" Wayne asked Cliff and Garret. "Maybe you two could join me for one of my hikes. Here's my card. Send me your e-mail and I'll let you know about the next couple of hikes."

Cliff nodded and took Wayne's card, glancing knowingly at Garret.

They all shook hands, and after Wayne took off, Cliff said, "I heard that his idea of a hike is actually mountain climbing—like climbing Mt. Olympus or Rainier. One guy told me he trained for weeks and he still couldn't keep up."

Garret laughed, his eyes widening. "You know, I've never lived near mountains before. Hiking in the mountains could give me a whole new take on physical fitness."

"For real. By the way, since you're into jazz, you oughta check out Tula's over there in Belltown. Julian Priester will be there next month," Cliff told him.

"Great! Man, he's world class. I heard him back in Chicago when I was just a kid."

"He's living here now. Tula's posts their schedule on the board outside. I could meet you there, and maybe get my brother to come. Here's my card. Give me a call one of these days and I'll give you a tour of the Central District."

"Shoot, man. I'll definitely take you up on that one." He handed Cliff one of his cards, too. "Far as I know, you're one of the first Seattle natives I've met since I got here."

Cliff looked knowingly at Garret as he gave him a brother's handshake.

As Ruthie walked into the Wild Ginger, she smelled the enticing aromas of fresh cilantro, lemongrass, shellfish, and stir-fry. Looking around, she saw that Fioretti was already at a table. She caught his eye, and he came over immediately and gave her a light peck on the cheek.

He was wearing a black suede shirt that fit in a way that suggested he may have been doing some body building over the last few years, and his hair was long and slicked back. She thought he looked like a member of the Wild Bunch, with that subtle intensity in his eyes that she had almost forgotten.

"You look stunning," he said and then leaned in to smell the side of her neck. "*Mm*, patchouli. I haven't smelled that for a long time."

She had forgotten how he pursed his lips together just slightly between words. He took her coat, hung it on the bamboo coat rack, and then lightly wrapped his arm around her waist, just long enough to peck her on the cheek again.

"It's nice to see you again, Fioretti." That was at least honest. She didn't feel like adding that he seemed even smoother now than he had before.

He led her back to his table and they sat down and ordered some drinks.

"This is a great menu. Look at these appetizers. Want to try some of the satays for starters?"

She nodded. "Absolutely."

"So. I was reading about your organization on the Web. You're a botanist for them? And a land steward? Very impressive. Of course, you have the background for something like that. It always amazed me, the way you could combine science and art. You were ahead of the rest of us, us—dilettantes."

She sipped some water. "I never saw it that way." She noticed two women at the table of four next to them. They were more dressed up than she was, both with low-cut dresses, and one had so much cleavage lined with strands of a black beaded necklace that her large breasts were almost entirely exposed. Ruthie certainly didn't feel overdressed in her jade green with the lace of her bra barely showing.

"Most of what I knew then was based on observation, whereas you and Isabelle and some of the others were erudite," she told him.

"But I didn't have the patience for academia," he said.

"So you started doing documentaries? I saw two of your films on PBS, which I thought were really good. I watched your last one with a friend of mine who's a filmmaker, and she liked your style. She described it as cinéma vérité."

"Thanks. Of course, some people say that we leave too much up to the viewer, that we need more narration."

"I tend to go for a more naturalistic style myself. Less manipulation."

"There's so much media hype around, that for me, the only way to try and counter it is to allow uncut interviews. Of course nobody wants to produce stuff that's that long."

"But when you do get on the air, you're reaching a whole lot of people, and your programs are international. What about the PBS station here in Seattle? Aren't they backing producers like you?"

"They used to," he said, shrugging. "But I heard the head guy blew all the station's money on HDTV production equipment so the station can barely afford to do much local production anymore."

"What a waste."

Fioretti nodded. "But, it looks like your organization's doing well? Working in about 30 countries now? To me, it's the international non-profit organizations that are just about our only hope. If there's a famine or a natural disaster in Africa or Asia or Latin America, who do you call? The government? Hell no. You call CARE or the Red Cross. The same holds true for wildlife poaching or human rights violations or medical emergencies. You call some non-profit, and they get their act over there while the rest of the world argues."

The people at the table next to them started giggling.

"Going international is keeping us from becoming complacent," Ruthie said, speaking more loudly. The volume in the room seemed to be cranking up.

The waiter brought the house wine and offered Fioretti a sip first.

"I'm sure it's fine," he said without tasting it. The waiter smiled and poured them two glasses.

"So here's to you, Ruthie—to a woman living according to the laws of nature!"

"Well thank you. I'd like to think that's true at least some of the time. But what's happened to you, Fioretti? Not even tasting the wine first? Your old arrogance, what's happened to it?" She held her breath for a moment when she realized she'd said exactly what she'd been thinking, but Fioretti just chuckled.

"I'm not sure. Maybe it's one too many overseas trips where the eye rolling got me in trouble. Or trying to speak English to someone who speaks it as a third language—the need for clarity? Sarcasm is the first thing to go. I was too busy trying to survive." Fioretti smiled. "But you, you could always outsmart me, Ruthie. Our innuendo was just posturing, the survival tactic of someone still learning the socio-political ropes of a large American high school. All of our so-called spontaneity was contrived, whereas you were somebody who could pull it off."

The waiter brought a variety of skewered satays, and they ordered phad thai and black cod for the main course.

"*Mm*, mushrooms and oysters! And this looks like zucchini." Fioretti offered her some from the platter and then took a plateful for himself.

"And where you come into the picture, I don't try and make excuses. There was one teacher at Roosevelt High School, a Native American man, who said that the way people act when they're a junior in high school pretty much foreshadows how they'll be for the rest of their lives. Of course, I didn't take him seriously then. I was too busy trying to prove myself as the Mediterranean male, trying to add another notch to my bow. The trouble is, I'm no archer."

"So you've really changed?" Ruthie asked, a little too eagerly, as she skewered a mushroom.

"For better or worse. My ego's been slapped around quite a bit. Work did some of that, especially when I was travelling. I don't know if you remember, but I was born in Italy." Ruthie nodded. "I decided to declare Italian citizenship, because it was easier to get visas with an Italian passport. There was too much at stake to behave like a total jerk. A jerk maybe, but not a *total* jerk."

Ruthie laughed, sipped the wine again and sampled the oysters. She rarely ate oysters, but these were delicious. Despite her best efforts to resist, she was actually starting to enjoy herself.

"But the thing about you, Ruthie, is you were a natural woman from the get-go. You were unpretentious, nothing seemed to faze you, and you were so versatile. Acting in plays, dancing, writing dynamite papers in school, running track. You seemed totally fearless, which is something that I've come to value. Compared to you, I was just an observer watching on the sidelines."

"But you were an intellectual with a capital *I*. I don't just mean smart. You remember Ed Doland? A 4.0 guy, but people said he acted like a robot, or that he *was* a robot. And Megan Shultz? If you asked her to read a poem out loud, it came out in a complete monotone. *Your* intellect was creative, and all over the map, and more about a personal quest. They got the grades, but they couldn't hold a candle to you."

Fioretti chuckled. "You always were a sweetheart, Ruthie." He leaned forward and looked at her with those intense eyes of his. "And I—I blew it with you. I'm sorry."

She felt warm all over. Almost transported. Almost as if they could recover lost time, or that time didn't even matter. She felt—exalted. For a moment, at least, she felt completely appreciated.

"Fioretti, you don't need to apologize. It was high school, for God's sake. They should say that all is fair in love and war, *and* high school. It was dog-eat-dog back then. And anyway," she said, looking down at her plate, "I believe you had a mission that involved several women."

"I think my mission was that I had to grow up. I can't blame my father, but he wasn't much help. Fortunately, my mother has a lot of backbone, along with a pretty robust intellect, which ultimately served me well. As I said, my ego got slapped around quite a bit, but even in those relationships I always wondered what was happening with Ruthie." There was something suggestive in the way he said her name.

"On the phone you said you didn't want to rekindle something from the past." It was a shame that she had to be so on guard, especially when a part of her was visualizing the two of them in candlelight—his tan body interlocked with hers in the act of forgiveness of all things past.

"Honestly, I don't. I wanted to get the past out of the way and apologize for the way I acted. But," he said, his eyes still intense, "I'd like to get to know you all over again, in the present. I'll be here for a couple of weeks at least—here, and in Vancouver. I'd like to see as much of you as possible."

Ruthie's thoughts started to spin. She tried to focus, but noticed that Fioretti was beginning to show the rough beginnings of a beard. She had to stop counting the ways in which this guy could turn her on.

"I'd like to take you to some nice places, if you can spare the time. To the beach, to some parks, maybe explore some of the places where you've been working."

It was all very tempting. She tried to stay reasonable. "Fioretti, I'm finding this a little hard to believe."

"It's all right, sweetheart. I probably deserve that." He looked down at his plate and she felt herself relax a little as she was released from the pull of his stare.

"This food is spectacular," he said casually.

He seemed to savor each morsel as he chewed. That was something he'd always seemed to have going for him, she remembered, that carpe diem attitude. As if the present moment were more important than the words he'd placed on the table just moments ago.

It was odd that he mentioned her living close to nature, considering they had never gotten that close—hadn't slept together. He had a way of stimulating a raw feeling in her—raw and unadulterated. A feeling like lying on a sandy beach, or sleeping in long grass, or wandering into a lush rain forest. He had charmed her in the past and he could charm her again. And she had little doubt that he knew it.

Watching him, she thought that his supposed recovery from sarcasm was probably just a subtler form of the old Fioretti. She wondered if much else had really changed. And for just a split second she felt a wave of compassion, even sympathy. Here he was, at the age of thirty, coming home and reaching out to a high school friend almost as if the relationships he had formed since then were meaningless. There was an incompleteness to him she couldn't quite fathom, perhaps the side of someone well-travelled that involved feeling rootless with only the slightest hint of being needy.

She could practically see his words, his offer, laid out on the table like an architectural model, waiting for her to shine her green light. But he could mean that he wanted a two-week casual affair. Surely he was capable of that, and she knew that she might be capable of that herself, with discipline. But she couldn't allow herself to become attached the way she had before. That would be devastating. She couldn't be the open book she had been before.

"I don't mean to spring something on you, Ruthie. But I've been thinking about this ever since you left New York and moved back here. I thought that maybe someone would fill the gap you left. That someone else would come along. But no one did. No one like you."

There was no misunderstanding that, she thought. She tried to savor each bite of the rest of her food, not knowing how to respond to him. Then she remembered that on her way to meet him, she'd imagined it could even be a business meeting—that he could be looking for people to invest in a movie and wanted suggestions from her. "So this really wasn't about fund raising for a documentary?" she asked.

He laughed again. "Would you cut that out?"

The waiter brought the bill, and Fioretti quickly reached into his wallet for his credit card. When they got up, he grabbed her coat and slipped it onto her shoulders. But this time, when he put his left hand around her waist, his thumb brushed her breast and she felt that warm tightness kindling between her legs in a way it hadn't in a long time. She knew this was going to be trouble.

"Let me walk you to your car," he said quietly. The way he steered her gently out the door then was smooth, but not pushy.

She was beginning to enjoy the attention, and having to analyze the sexual politics of every move he made was beginning to feel tedious.

When they reached her car, he asked if she'd like to see his parents' new house where he was staying in Ravenna. It really wasn't out of her way, and she didn't feel like judging whether he was leading to something decadent. Maybe he was just wearing her down, but she was getting tired of being on guard. Tired of evaluating his every move. After all, she was capable of behaving without strings attached.

It dawned on her then that maybe she had grown up a little.

Chapter Six

†

The morning after the foundation dinner, Garret got to the office early and went to the food court at the bottom level of his building. He picked up a paper, got a latte and a bagel, and sat in the deserted sunken section near the big waterfall that drowned out most of the noise around him.

As he started reading his paper he heard bird song. At first he thought it was part of the sound system, but when he glanced around he saw that it was a real live bird, maybe a sparrow, singing away on the floor under one of the tables. No one else seemed to be paying any attention to it. He wondered how it had gotten inside, and how long it would be before it realized it was stuck and went into a panic.

As he took the elevator up to the top floor, he debated who he should call to come and rescue the bird. The city parks department? Or maybe just the manager of the building?

When he got to his desk there was a one-page fax waiting from Dan Gibbs, addressed to both him and Ruthie:

"Dear Ms. Adams and Mr. Carter: We regret to inform you that Mr. Arnie McGowan passed away on Thursday of last week, March 28th. You are advised expressly not to contact Mrs. McGowan or any other family members during this period of grieving.

Yours truly, Daniel Gibbs, Esquire"

Garret felt a sinking feeling in his stomach. He remembered Arnie in that house more than two months ago—his emaciated body, his very white skin, so thin it was almost translucent. Arnie had been so weak then, but Garret realized he hadn't really believed he was dying. He had wanted to believe that Arnie would see the day that his property was saved from development. He'd wanted to believe that Arnie would walk on it again, knowing it would be protected for good.

He had believed in the word *remission.*

He dialed Ruthie. "Ruthie, did you get the fax?" he asked when she answered.

"Yup. It's here." Her voice sounded faint.

"I'm sorry it happened so suddenly. I—I honestly didn't expect this." He took a slow breath. "I realize you've lost a good friend."

"Well, it feels really—sudden. Like… I was cut off at the end."

Garret listened to her breath on the other end of the line. She was too strong a woman to get emotional, but he could hear her disappointment. "Something about all this doesn't feel right," she added, pausing again. "Even besides the son-in-law's wacko attitude. The tone of it sounds like a power trip. And it doesn't mention anything about a memorial service."

"I don't know—I still can't read this guy Dan. Maybe he's just trying to handle things so Arnie's wife doesn't have to. But he's taking his role incredibly seriously."

"Garret, if there's a memorial service, will you go with me?"

"Of course, you got it. And—" he tried to keep his voice strong and even, "try not to feel bad. This all may seem abrupt, but unfortunately, clients do die. And sometimes it happens when you're right in the middle of something important. At least his donation should be protected by the will."

A few days later, Ruthie called and said there was an obituary for Arnie in the morning paper, and that a service was being held in Bellingham. "But it doesn't say where," she added.

"Well, I suppose if they want to have a small private family service without publishing the location, then that's their business."

"All right. It's just so awkward for our organization—not just me personally—to have a wedge put between us and this family. It's the opposite of how we want to do things when someone cares enough to donate land to us."

"Of course. You'd much rather have buy-in from the family with a donation like this."

"I think I need to distract myself from this limbo and this sadness. It's not my job to feel personally rejected. That's sort of an ego trip in itself. Remember when I told you I was taking a flamenco dance class? Well, tomorrow we're having a guest instructor who's going to show us a few salsa dances. They told us to bring a partner, and I was wondering... How would you like to join me?"

"Sounds like fun! But I have to warn you, I'm no dancer." He thought it would be great to do something with her that didn't involve work. But he didn't want to sound too excited.

"They say you don't need any experience for the class. It's just an introduction, to give us a break from all this flamenco." She explained it was a few blocks from her office and she'd meet him there.

"Okay, folks. We're going to start out simple here with a basic rumba." Miguel, the guest instructor, projected his voice loudly across the room. "The rumba is the foundation for all the Cuban dances. Carmelita and I," he said, gesturing at the attractive woman next to him, "will give you a demonstration. We're starting off with some Mongo Santamaría. Ready? Watch our feet!"

The dancers' footwork was so quick, Garret couldn't follow what they were doing. And their bodies were very loose: their hips, their shoulders, everything seemed to move independently.

"See how close the steps are to the lead drum part?" Miguel said as he moved with Carmelita across the floor. "You can see the connection between rumba and flamenco. Rumba is the blend of flamenco with African sacred dances."

When the next piece started, Miguel told the class to try it. "Go for it! Don't worry about any specific steps. Just let your feet move with that lead drummer and the beat will take you there!"

Garret had never tried the rumba before, but he had played these rhythms back in college, with a band that played Afro-Cuban stuff. He took Ruthie's hand somewhat cautiously, and somebody in the class asked why the rumbas were called rest dances.

"Back in Cuba the slaves were only allowed to dance on Sunday, the day of rest, the only day that they didn't work," Miguel explained. "Unlike those in the United States, African slaves in Cuba retained their drums. So they retained some of their dances. Ah! That's right! Move those hips! Loosen those joints! No holding back! Each time you move your feet, it counts!"

The instructor twirled around the room while holding onto his partner, coaching each couple all the while. Garret had watched mambos, rumbas. He had seen really good Latin dancing and he knew it could take years to make this all seem effortless.

"Now drop!" Miguel shouted. Luckily, Garret had worn his loafers, which were pretty soft. He didn't want to be stomping all over Ruthie.

After a few dances they took a break and went over to the side for some water.

"Garret, you're doing great! I knew you'd be good. It's like playing an instrument, only you use your body for the riffs."

He could feel the energy pulsing from her—the kind that only music and dancing created. Her eyes were shining, with that warmth he'd noticed when he first met her.

"Well, like I said, I'm no dancer. Some of these guys are really talented." He found a small towel and wiped his forehead. He had worked up a little sweat.

"When I lived in New York City, we danced all the time," she told him, her tone easy and light. "A lot of parties with NuYoricans and Afro-Caribbeans. And we'd dance for awhile, take a break and talk, dance some more. And, you know, it kept you active."

She smiled as she started to catch her breath. "That's why I took the class this winter, so I'd keep moving."

Garret remembered that she'd said she had worked for the botanical garden in New York before coming back to the Northwest, and that many of her relatives on her father's side were Romani. She took one of the towels and wiped around her neck. While she was looking away, he took a moment to study her. Dancing fit the willowiness of her body—her long legs, hand gestures that practically told stories by themselves, the firm roundness of her breasts. There was something incredibly sensual about a woman who could dance.

They tried a few other dances—the mambo, the cha cha, the congo, and the tango. But Miguel kept emphasizing that the rumba was the basis of all the Afro-Cuban dances, and that the basic clave beat was at the heart of it. Garret bumped into Ruthie's toes a few times, but she just giggled quietly. And as for the dips backward, she was incredibly flexible and he was strong enough to hold her, so she dropped backward farther than anyone else in the class.

When they finally left the dance studio, it was past 9:30 p.m. He suggested they go get some dinner and she agreed. They headed over to Mama's, the Mexican place in Belltown, and sat in the room that was all decked out with Elvis memorabilia. An odd choice for décor, Garret thought.

"Man, after that, I'm starving! You can burn up a lot of juice doing that," he told her.

Her lips had a sort of heart shape to them that he had never noticed before. And those big bright brown eyes and that black curly hair… Man, she was really something.

"You know, Ruthie, it's nice to share something with you that's not related to work."

She nodded. "I know what you mean. That was a great workout, thanks for doing it. I could tell you're a musician by the way you moved your body."

He thought he saw her blush, but he wasn't sure. Somebody was playing mariachi music on the jukebox in the other room.

"Have you done a lot of singing? Your voice has a melodious quality," he said as they opened their menus.

Ruthie laughed. "Not really. I took a couple of acting classes that might have done something. For awhile, I was trying to decide if I should be a drama and dance major, or do botany. But I ended up combining them. I guess I'm sort of non-confrontational by nature, so I chose to blend things. But I couldn't predict where one path might take me."

"For instance?"

"Well, I had a job down in Oregon, working for the state game department for a while, during the days of the spotted owl inventories. It was a harmless job, really. I just went into certain land holdings and counted the owls. The only thing I really had to be careful about was not to double count, and I enjoyed it. A very peaceful job at first. It gave me a chance to see what was left of the forests down there, and I got pretty good at tree climbing."

The waiter brought chips and salsa, and they put in their orders.

"So you were saying—you didn't run into many people on this job?"

"Not at first. But some of the state lands bordered on private lands, so I'd occasionally run into people who were mending fences or doing some scouting before hunting season. Well, one day this guy with a rifle over his shoulder showed up and asked me what I was doing. When I told him the purpose of my work, expecting him to relax about me being there, he told me to get the hell out of there or he'd give me something to remember and pulled his gun off his shoulder. Of course, I left that site and didn't go back! But to be honest, I thought he was just a crazy, that it was a fluke. And I was determined to finish the job.

"A couple weeks later, I was on another site, scoping things out from up in a tree. When I climbed down, this younger guy appeared all of a sudden. He asked me if I was looking for spotted owls and I said yes. He held a gun up to my face, looked me straight in the eye, and told me to quit or he'd kill me."

"No shit. Just for counting birds?"

"Yup. The owls had become a symbol of loggers losing control of their land. For many of them, logging was a way of life, and I think you have to believe that for any of this to make sense. When that happened, I realized it was pretty arrogant for people in the environmental movement to come along and say that logging had to stop, when there were really no viable job alternatives. We were naïve back then—we may still be. I like to think that we learned from that and are helping to create new jobs, like tree thinning and planting, road decommissioning, building trails, even helping with new culverts so they're fish-friendly. I called my boss and told him what was going on and he told me to stop, that it was too risky in there. A few weeks after that, we learned that somebody discovered some big patches of marijuana growing down there." The waiter brought their plates which, he said, were very hot.

"Oh, so these guys could have been protecting their crops?"

"Maybe so. It's hard to tell what's really going on in all those thick woods. They've loosened the laws now in Oregon, but at the time they were passing out some pretty stiff sentences for growing plants. Not long after that, the opening came up at the botanical garden in New York. I was ready for a change so I took the job. It felt so cultured there. Everything was about preservation—preserving the city, preserving the beauty—it wasn't about a fight. At least my job wasn't." She took a sip of her beer and glanced down, almost shyly. She looked vulnerable then, and he felt an urge to kiss her.

"Shucks, I never heard of anybody moving to New York to get away from crime."

Ruthie laughed. "Life is full of so many ironies. This is great Mexican food, by the way. Really hits the spot!"

He drove her home to the little bungalow in Fremont that she shared with another woman. She told him that she had a pretty good-sized garden in back, and in her case, he believed it.

"Garret, you've been great. Thanks so much for coming. It was really fun." She paused for a moment before adding, "I'd invite you in, but my roommate is still unpacking and things are scattered all over the place."

"Hey, no problem. Let's do this again. Man, you're such a versatile lady! And brave too, with that owl business. I never thought… " His voice dropped.

He couldn't find the words to describe what he wanted to say—that he'd somehow never thought that she'd been put to the test the way she had. At least, he couldn't find a way to say it without sounding naïve, and possibly sexist. So he just said, "You seem totally dedicated to your work," which he now knew was an understatement.

"Thanks," she said and grinned. "Tomorrow I'm heading up to the Skagit for a little while." She took out a card and wrote a phone number on the back of it. "Here's the phone number for the cabin where I'll be staying. You can't count on cell phones up there. Let me know if you hear anything from Arnie's son-in-law, okay?" She squeezed his forearm as she got out of the car.

He had an odd feeling as he crossed the Fremont Bridge—almost like he was disappointed she was going to be out of town, disappointed that he wasn't going to see her for a few days. And here she was heading north, and he hadn't even asked how long she'd be up there.

He had liked her before because she seemed so steady, strong emotionally but still warm. He had liked her because he thought he could believe in her as a colleague, as someone he could trust. But now he liked her because he knew she had gone to the mat and had come through intact, and because she was willing to submit herself to an art form, to dance. She was willing to expose herself and that took guts.

After enduring the dance class together, it wouldn't be off the wall to ask her out, he decided as he drove home. And that was all the more reason to close this land deal.

When he got home he put on a Santana album. He put away the photo of Jackie and himself at Lake Michigan and hung the photo Ruthie sent him of the eagles on the Skagit. He realized he didn't even know if Ruthie was in a relationship.

In less than two months, he'd been introduced to eagles and mountains, salmon and old growth forests, and, of course, some intriguing people. He just couldn't quite figure out what dues he was supposed to be paying.

The Arnie McGowan case was a true litmus test now. If he looked at it objectively, he knew he had already suffered two strikes: not being able to deal with the son-in-law man-to-man, and having Arnie die before the transfer documents got signed. At this point he couldn't prove that the bank had helped the case along at all. And now Sybil could argue that his failure to get a meeting with the CPA was strike three.

The following Monday Garret got a call from Vance who reminded him they had plans to hook up at Tula's for an evening gig and open mike.

When he got to the club, things were already popping: Julian Priester on trombone, Hadley Caliman on tenor sax, and some other folks on bass, piano, and drums playing one of Bird's tunes. The place was filling up, and he found Vance and Nadine at a table near the bandstand.

"Man—way to go Garret! They just started," Vance told him.

"Hey, you two," he said, sliding into a chair.

Their table was next to some autographed photos on the wall—Sonny Rollins, Dizzy Gillespie, Miles. It was a small place, with a lot of tables, semi-jammed together and forming a wide L around the stage. A bar was tucked toward the back. Caliman was cutting up on his tenor, and Priester countered with an incredibly warm soothing tone like no trombone Garret had ever heard.

"Priester played with Sun Ra way back when, back in Chicago!" Vance almost shouted.

The woman on piano was also strong, working with a young looking kid on drums. The bass player had a smooth richness that glued it all together.

Garret couldn't remember exactly how old he was when he first heard Priester with his parents, at some bar on the south side of Chicago that let in kids during the early set. It was definitely way back when he was in elementary school. He had heard jazz before on concert stages, but hearing the music that time was different—so loose and natural and free. The players had given each other lots of space to take solos and let the set go as long as they wanted. When his dad really got into a set, like he had that night, he let you know about it. He shouted "Yeah!" after some tasty solo and whistled loud during the applause.

His parents had no set religion, but in those places, on those few special nights, they were in church.

Priester's speaking voice was subdued. He introduced the piano player, Jessica Williams, and she played a florid introduction to the tune "For All We Know," a tune Garret had played at a gala concert on Mother's Day his senior year in high school.

It had been another big solo he'd taken for granted, while other band members competed for them. He'd gotten loaded before the gig. Back then he thought he sounded better when he smoked reefer. His mom had said something about smelling reefer; he knew she could tell because of the way he seemed to run out of air while he was playing his horn. But he told her it was coming from the girls' bathroom.

"I put my name on the open mike list," Vance told him. "You down with adding yours?"

"Nah, I've got no axe, man, and you know I'm still rusty," Garret said.

"I'm sure you could get your lips around a mouthpiece just like always."

Garret took a sip of his ginger ale. "One of these days."

"I'd love to hear you play," Nadine said. "Both of you. Actually, Vance has been practicing a lot lately, in the evenings. Or so he tells me." She winked at her fiancé.

"Nothing like music to keep you focused when your hope-to-die is out there working late at school."

Garret knew that Nadine had been working even longer hours than before, but Vance was too positive a brother to complain while everybody was having fun.

The next tune was a loud up-tempo thing that sounded like something by the Art Ensemble of Chicago. Jessica Williams played percussively, like drops of water pattering down on a river. The drummer was adding textures—layering sounds like changes in landscapes and altitudes, building a framework like geological formations, like the layers of mountains up on the Skagit. The kid was versatile, shifting gears at a moment's notice, catching cues from the other musicians. Priester introduced each band member, including the young drummer who was filling in and doing an awesome job—a high school kid named Kassa.

They broke for intermission and Vance went up to the bandstand and introduced himself to the bass player.

"That was beautiful!" Nadine said enthusiastically to Garret. "Lots of times, I forget that Seattle has some real world class players who've chosen to live here."

"Yea—no kidding!" Garret recognized the dude standing near-by and waved him over. "Cliff! Hey, man, what's up?"

"How you doin'? I just got here. How was the first set?"

"It was crackin'. Have a seat! Cliff, this is my friend Nadine Hathaway, and that's my buddy Vance up there, talkin' with the bass player. Yeah, they're great. What do you want? We just ordered a pitcher and some glasses for now."

"Yeah, a little brew is fine for me," he said, relaxing into a seat.

Vance came back to the table looking fired up, and shook Cliff's hand as Garret introduced them. "I gave my card to Buddy Catlett, the bass player," he said, grinning. "I'm thinking about taking a few lessons from him to help me get my chops back."

The musicians came back and started playing a Dexter Gordon tune that featured Caliman's rich smooth tenor sax and a student of his named Carlos—also on tenor—who wove in and out with some tasty riffs. Then Priester played one of his originals, swapping fours with Caliman. They ended the set with a Coltrane tune, "Impressions," that gave the drummer room for a long solo.

"I can't remember when I've heard such a well-rounded bunch of musicians," Garret said as the applause died down. The place was still full, and people were ordering plates of food.

Priester announced that it was time for open mike. The first act up was a group of his students from Cornish, the local arts college, who made nice work of a couple of Thelonious Monk tunes, "In Walked Bud" and "Ruby My Dear," which Monk had written when he was only thirteen.

Then Catlett invited Vance to the stage. Vance told them he wanted to play Monk's "Well You Needn't," and the tenor man switched over to the soprano sax. Garret leaned back into his seat to watch his buddy, but then Vance said something to the sax player, and the next thing Garret knew he was motioning him onto the stage.

"Hey man, I've got an extra mouthpiece you can use," the horn player told him.

It was almost more work to protest.

Garret adjusted the reed and before he knew it they were off and running on "Well You Needn't," with their two horns playing the head in unison. He dropped out to let the guy take a solo on his soprano, and then Vance played around with the head and the baseline the way he used to like there was no tomorrow. When he nodded at Garret, Garret stepped back in, hesitant at first, but the drummer egged him on.

He thought of Carmen McRae's lyrics—*you're actin' sincere, well you needn't, you're callin' me dear, well you needn't*—and an incredible feeling of warmth came over him so he was glad he had gotten up there even though he was rusty because the deal was, he realized as he played, you gotta do your life no matter what, you gotta tell your own story and sometimes you gotta go find it, dig it out from somewhere it's been buried, sometimes you gotta scream for it just to find it, he thought as the horn wailed, because jazz wasn't just his parents' music, it belonged to a whole universe, belonged to the sky and the clouds and the trees and the river, belonged to saintly folks like Monk and Coltrane and Miles, and to plain folks like him and Ruthie and Arnie McGowan and to the gods, to future unborn children and to whoever would hear it and he sailed through another round of changes, and then he noticed his solo was getting a little long, so he managed to fade in sync with the changes and turned to the piano player and she smiled at him and rounded out the phrase, the drummer put in a tasty little punctuating roll, Garret took a quick nod and got a loud applause.

The piano player took her version and then Garret and the horn player came back in with the head in unison and the crowd roared.

Catlett motioned to Vance and Garret to do another tune, but Vance said he was smart enough to quit while he was ahead and Garret felt the same way, so he smiled and set the dude's horn back onto the stand.

When they were back at the table, Nadine patted Garret on the back and gave Vance a kiss.

"I could listen to you dudes all day," Cliff told them.

As they listened to the rest of the set, Garret thought about how long he had been putting off getting back into the music. When he'd decided not to major in music back in college, it was because he thought he needed to have something to fall back on, something more "real"—that old cliché. But why did that *something* have to consume his entire life? Why had he let it extinguish the music? In high school, he'd known that becoming a pro in music meant you had to invest a ton of time, day in and day out practices and getting to gigs, keeping a balance between the two so that you didn't play the same licks all the time. He'd decided there had to be an easier way to make a living, especially a good living, and had ended up choosing all those years in law school and then working at banks.

But what if he had put that much time into music instead, what would have happened then? Would he feel better about himself? And not have to deal with total disasters like this character Dan Gibbs?

Cliff talked about his brother Dirk, who was the only family man out of their crew, and was coaching Little League. Looking at Garret and Vance he asked, "You two ever thought about doing any coaching?"

They both hemmed and hawed. Vance's excuse was his commute to the Eastside was messing up his schedule.

"Not that I'm trying to twist your arm. Just think about it 'cause we'll always have need for brothers like you." Garret compromised and said he might be ready to be an assistant coach in a few weeks.

The next morning at work, Garret was in the file room doing research on a client. Suddenly he heard commotion in the lunchroom and walked in to check it out as several others clustered in, including his boss Sybil. A woman turned up the TV in the back of the room. "There's been a shooting at some high school in Jefferson County!" she shouted.

"Jefferson County? That's over on the Olympic Peninsula!"

People were crowding around the set. "Wait—it's Jefferson County in Colorado!" someone yelled.

Twelve people had been killed in a high school called Columbine outside of Denver, in a town called Littleton. As they watched the screen, a news anchor reported that two students with automatic weapons had gone on a wild shooting rampage—killing twelve other students, a teacher, and then themselves. The images were mostly of the chaos at the scene, a few reporters firing questions at cops and school administrators, and perhaps most disturbing, someone's video footage of it actually happening. One reporter said that a video monitor at the school showed someone bringing a weapon into the building, but that no one had seen it until after the shooting. The screen changed, showing an interview of the school principal and a gun control advocate.

"Can you imagine that?" Sybil asked. "Right in a high school? I guess you're not safe anywhere." At first, no one could find the words to answer her.

"You can't be complacent, not even for a minute," Garret said finally. "How do high school kids get their hands on weapons like that and not have somebody find out about it?" When he was in high school he had stashed a gun he was holding for his wanna-be friend down in his parents' basement. But his dad found it and got rid of it.

The room kept filling up and people watched, some commenting but most stunned and subdued by the news. Two staff members said they had relatives who lived near Littleton, the town in Colorado.

When Garret got home that night he tuned into CNN and watched a few interviews with the parents of the kids who'd been killed. One of them, a father who was visibly distraught and angry, said he had already written to Charlton Heston, president of the NRA, even before this happened. He said he hadn't gotten a response then, and he hadn't gotten one now, and he planned to picket the NRA. "I know who killed my son," he said. "But the NRA is responsible for blocking the Brady Bill and allowing kids in schools to get guns. I'm not going to sit back and watch more people die from gun violence, not if I can do something."

Garret went to the bedroom closet where his saxophone was stashed. His father had insisted that he bring it to Seattle, even though Garret hadn't been sure he would even play it. "Don't you be forgetting where you come from, son," his father had said sternly.

He still had the soft duster that cleaned out the inside of the horn, and he pulled it out now. The tune his dad used to warm up on back in the day was "Moanin" by Bobby Timmons, which sounded like an old black spiritual, and he thought of all the parents of the Columbine high school kids as he noodled around on that tune. As he played, he thought of the lyrics by Jon Hendricks, a few he could remember, that went something like:

> Every mornin' finds me moanin', yes Lord,
>
> 'cause of all the trouble I see, yes Lord.
>
> Life's a losin' gamble to me, yes Lord. Lord I try, I really truly try
>
> To find some relief, find some relief.
>
> Lord I spend plenty days and nights alone with my grief, alone with my grief.
>
> Every evening's got me moanin', yes Lord, all alone and cryin' the blues,
>
> I'm so tired of payin' these dues.
>
> Yes, I'm tired, I'm really truly tired of paying these dues, really payin' these dues.
>
> Lord I'm paying, I'm really truly paying, truly payin' these dues.
>
> Lord I pray, I really truly pray somebody will come and remedy me.

> Lord I pray, I really truly pray, Lord I pray, I truly really pray.
>
> Truly I pray, Lord I really pray, really I pray, Lord I pray true.
>
> I truly really pray, pray, I Lord…

He thought about calling his parents, though it was pretty late in Chicago. And he liked to call when he had some good news to report. After all, he was an adult and they had stopped trying to give him advice.

He could call Ruthie, but there wasn't much to talk about now except Columbine, and that was a downer. He wished he had a reason to call, like news from the CPA, but he didn't have any.

At least he knew she was somewhere safe.

Chapter Seven

†

The following Monday morning Garret woke up to loud chirping from outside that made him want to open his window all the way. As fresh air moved into the room he noticed a fragrance he hadn't smelled in Seattle before, a pungent pollen scent that reminded him of early Midwest summers, with their warm lazy breezes.

Suddenly, he remembered the dream he'd been having right before he woke up.

He was swimming in a river, against the current. On the side of the river was a gravel bar, and the dude who sold the homeless newspaper was standing on it. He kept pointing to the headlines of the paper, but Garret couldn't see them. Up ahead, he saw Ruthie waving. Switching from a breaststroke to a crawl, he started to overtake the current. But then he came to another gravel bar. His boss Sybil was there, talking with Dan Gibbs, and as he got closer, Dan pointed at him and guffawed loudly.

Garret wasn't sure if it was the radio DJ providing the material for Dan's laughter or the birds singing so loudly outside that had jarred him awake.

He didn't take his dreams all that seriously. There was nothing revealing in that one anyway—except that Jackie wasn't in it. And that it took place now, in the present, with Ruthie waving him in to shore. All right, he conceded. Maybe there was something to it, but he didn't want his fantasy life getting ahead of what was really happening. He was thirty now; it was too late in his life for that kind of immature stuff. He didn't even know if she had a boyfriend.

On his walk to work, the air was balmy, heavy and still, thick and intoxicating. The waterfront, blue and sparkly, was nearly free of mist, and in the bushes in the small park on Third the crows were making a racket so loud it nearly drowned out the passing cars. For the first time, he noticed a long row of daffodils blooming along the border. They seemed unnaturally, incredibly yellow. Only then did it strike him what was so different about the day: it was sunny.

Maybe he could go up to the Skagit and take Ruthie to dinner. He could spend the night somewhere, a hotel, so she wouldn't feel like he was coming on too strong. After that dance class, it was his move.

At the corner by the bank building, a young Asian woman was selling mixed bouquets of daffodils, tulips and other bright flowers with a sweet fragrance like cloves. There was a light airiness to the city now that the sun had shown itself—people smiled and gestured as they talked, pausing to let others walk by. A handful of folks were standing in front of the dreadlocks brother as he rapped one of his standard rhymes.

"If you're not lame, you'll read Real Change, it won't give you wealth or give you fame, but reveal the truth about Y2K …" He put some beats in the middle, sold some papers, and went on: "With the poor gettin' poorer and the rich gettin' richer, the brokers won't jump unless there's a ticker." Somebody handed the dude a latte.

When Garret got to his office, the receptionist followed him in with a big bouquet of flowers and a note from the building management. "Thanks for calling us about the stray bird. We released it right away," he read off the card.

As she left, she added, "And there's a woman in the lobby who said she wants to make an appointment with you."

He walked out to the lobby and found a young woman rummaging through a large briefcase. She slowly stood up when she saw him, a little nervously, and held out her hand.

"Hi. I'm Diane Gibbs. You may not remember me, but we met at the bar association luncheon a few weeks ago."

He vaguely remembered being introduced to a tall blond woman who might have looked like her, but the woman hadn't said much. "Well, it's nice to see you again. What can I do for you?"

"I'm looking for some legal advice."

"Sure, why don't you come on down to my office."

He directed her into the office, relieved he hadn't thrown any files on the armchair. He noticed that the peach color of her flower print dress matched some of his tulips. As she sat down, she looked around cautiously.

"It's about my father—Arnie McGowan."

Garret coughed. "Oh—I'm sorry. I didn't recognize your name at first," he said, closing the door.

"Aren't you the man who met my folks a couple of months ago, back in February, along with the woman from the conservation group?"

"That's right. I enjoyed meeting your folks a lot. They seemed like great people. I was very sorry to hear about your father."

"Well, thanks." She looked down.

Garret couldn't get a read on her, but something was obviously bothering her. "Say, how about some coffee?" he offered, to help put her at ease. "We could have it brought in."

"Oh, no, I'm fine for now. Thanks." She smiled then, but he could still feel a weight resting on her mind as she sighed and leaned back in the chair. "Mr. Carter, I apologize for not calling first. It was difficult for me to decide to come down today." She cleared her throat. "Have you read my father's will?"

"No, not yet." Garret was starting to get the feeling that this conversation might not be going in the best direction.

"Okay, well, I can save you a trip to the courthouse." She dug into her briefcase and handed him a will about five pages thick. As he started to leaf through it she said, "The part about the Skagit property is on page three. It says that it goes to the conservation group if my mother dies within sixty days of my father's death, but… if not, well, it goes to my mother as far as I can tell."

"Oh, no kidding?" He turned to the third page and read it over. "Yup. It goes to your mom. No charitable gift involved. Shucks... Diane, I don't want to speak out of turn, but the Conservancy is going to be really disappointed. The idea was for that property to serve as a link between some conserved public land and a large commercial forest that may be placed under some kind of sustainable logging agreement. Of course, it's pretty common to give property to a spouse like this, but it's not the assumption we were operating under—especially since your dad turned over the keys and the deeds to the group and gave them permission to access the property."

Garret shook his head and tried to keep his voice neutral. "It seemed really important to him to get this done. But you're right." He glanced over the page again. "There's really no equivocating in the way this will is worded. Giving the land to charity would be contingent upon your mother dying within sixty days of your father's death. Unless …" he hesitated. "Unless she decides to donate it to the Conservancy herself."

"This really sucks." Diane was still holding the briefcase in her lap and gripped it tightly. "My father always said the will was worded so that land would go to conservation. And I thought my husband Dan agreed. He never mentioned any kind of contingency and—I didn't look it over myself. After all, he was my husband and a lawyer."

Garret couldn't help but notice that she'd put a certain amount of weight on the word *was*.

"I trusted him—trusted him to do what my dad wanted. If my dad even read that will, I doubt the word 'contingent' would have meant anything to him anyway. My dad said he was donating the land to the conservation group. Period. And in exchange, they were going to pay Mom income from some annuity thing. It was like an installment sale, only she was going to get income for her whole life."

Garret searched for the right words, but Diane wasn't finished talking.

"Let's face it, Mr. Carter," she said, leaning forward in her chair. "My husband sabotaged my dad's ability to conserve this land, to give it to posterity." She had a determined look; she seemed more indignant than victimized now, yet her eyes brimmed slightly with tears as she looked at him.

Garret handed her a box of tissues and looked down at the will again. "Well, I can totally see why it was hard for you to come down here today."

"You probably don't know the half of it." She set the briefcase on the floor and blew her nose. "My father wanted to do something special with that property. I told my husband he was ignoring my father's wishes," she said, stuffing the tissue into the pocket of her dress. "He just laughed. Told me I didn't have a clue about what was really going on. But Mr. Carter, it was Dan who didn't understand my father. Dan just humored him. Maybe he was just humoring me, too. And my mom, well, I can't get her to talk about it now, she's so numb."

"It looks like it's in her hands now—whatever happens."

"And you don't think the Conservancy will object?"

"Honestly, I'm not sure. The way I see it, it would be hard to prove your father didn't understand how the will was worded. A judge might ask why, if this donation was so definite, why didn't the bank get the transfer documents signed before your father got so sick. The evidence may not be clear that it was Dan who blocked this deal. At least that's my take on first blush."

"Okay, maybe I can't ask you to fight that battle. No offense, but fighting with a damn lawyer can be impossible. Dan knew what he was doing. I'm not asking you to represent me, but…" She took a deep breath. "Do you know a good divorce lawyer?"

"Well, there's the bar association list… I have it here in my files. I'll make you a copy. I'm sorry—is this for you?" He felt obligated to ask, to present his neutral position.

"Of course. The guy's losing it. He's changed. I can't figure out why he does half the things he does. What he did to my father is unforgivable, and I'm not sitting still for it."

"Diane, it's a peculiar thing. Greed can drive people in outrageous directions. I can't say for sure, but he may have seen this property as your inheritance."

"Sure he did. My inheritance and, more to the point, his." She grabbed another tissue and wiped her eyes. "You may not know that I have a brother, too. Well, Dan contributed to his becoming alienated from my parents. It's my fault—I should have seen what was going on. But, I had my life, my teaching job—I wasn't watching. I didn't stop to look at the deeper side of what Dan was up to. And, of course, he's got himself down as executor of Dad's estate along with me."

"Well, if you get a divorce, you might be able to petition the court for a change. You could talk with your lawyer about it." Garret knew he had to be careful. What if there was some sort of court case around all this and he had to represent the Conservancy? He couldn't be giving her legal advice.

"Okay, I'll do it. I've got a lot to set in motion. I'm still in shock over all this, over what this represents about Dan. And I need to get out to the property to check on things. Dad and I were going to go together, but I kept putting it off thinking that one of these days he would feel better." At that, she started getting choked up again. Garret waited while she steadied herself. Finally she said, "Maybe if I could get my mom out there, it would remind her of what Dad was trying to do."

"Hold on and I'll make you a copy of this list," he said.

As he walked to the copy room, he could feel sweat dripping from his underarms. He felt worked up. He knew there had to be more questions he should be asking right now.

He loaded the copier and pushed the start button. Blank pages shot out, and he realized he had put the sheets in face down, the way it worked at his old job. What was wrong with him? He reloaded the pages.

He was letting himself get thrown off balance by a horrendous jerk, and all the while trying to impress Ruthie and his boss and his co-workers, not to mention his clients. It was too much. And now this woman—Diane. The grieving daughter. How did he know he could trust her? His gut told him she wasn't acting, but right now that was all he had to go on. With the Conservancy as his client, he felt justified talking with her about Arnie's will, and if the Conservancy did have a lawsuit she could be their best witness. He grabbed the copies and a got a couple glasses of ice water to take back with him.

Back in the office, Diane seemed to have calmed down and thanked him. "I've got a lot to do this week, but I'm thinking about going up on Friday with my mom. I'd be happy to have you join me if you'd like. Not as my lawyer of course, but in your role representing the Conservancy."

"If you feel comfortable doing it that way, I don't think it would hurt. I was planning to go up there to meet with Ruth anyway. She's working up there near your property right now. This is all in your mother's hands now, and she certainly has a right to see what kind of conservation work is going on up there."

As soon as the words were out of his mouth, he realized he might have just blown the fantasy of spending the night over a nice dinner with Ruthie, and hanging out with her the next day.

Quickly, he groped for a way to fix it. "I'd be happy to give you both a ride up, but I may be spending the night up at the Skagit. If you don't mind catching a bus back? I could get you to Mount Vernon if there's nothing closer."

"Oh, that's fine." She didn't seem to notice that the situation had him flustered. "Of course..." She looked at him as if suddenly remembering something crucial. "This is all strictly confidential. Even if someone calls you pretending to be my lawyer, don't speak to them unless you hear from me. I need to make a clean break, and I don't want *anyone* interfering."

"I understand." He nodded, but he knew there was a lot he didn't understand.

She handed him a card with her cell phone number and suggested meeting at the Monorail Espresso downtown on Friday morning.

As he walked her to the lobby, she seemed determined, even energized. Who could say how it would play out? Maybe she really would take her ex-husband to court. A good lawyer might be able to come up with a case showing Gibbs had manipulated her father's will. Even though Ruthie had to return the keys and the deeds, there was evidence in Gibbs's fax that Arnie had turned them over to the Conservancy. Why hadn't a lawyer outside the family, an impartial party, reviewed the will to see if it followed Arnie's wishes? As Larry had said, it was all too close for comfort.

That night he called Ruthie. She told him she was staying at a friend's cottage on the Sauk River near the Skagit, a real rustic getaway. She was working with the eagle census data. He told her about his talk with Diane Gibbs, Arnie's will, and that it sounded like Diane was planning to divorce Dan. He mentioned that it sounded like they had been estranged, or close to it, for some time.

"Damn! I guess we're not the only ones who think this guy is weird."

"I know. But, Ruthie? Remember that after someone dies, people tend to get emotional. The grief period is such a volatile time. She may wind up forgiving Dan, accepting that it's her mom's property now, and that it's up to her to decide what to do with it. More than anything, she's stunned. With the uncertainty over all of this, getting Mrs. McGowan up on the property may help." Ruthie sighed in agreement. "Do you think you could meet us there? I figure we'll arrive between eleven and noon, but I can give you a call when we're close."

"I suppose it's the best we can do right now," Ruthie said, sounding disappointed.

"This is an odd one, Ruthie, very odd, but Diane may be able to turn this around. And if not, well," he took a quick breath, "it won't be a wasted trip. I'd like to see you again anyway, take you somewhere for a nice dinner, and maybe go for a hike on Saturday?"

"Good. Ok, I'll be at the McGowan place between eleven and noon. Cell phones up here can be very iffy, so keep this number—the one you dialed—it's the land line at the cabin," she said, and they hung up.

Yes! He felt like celebrating. She agreed to something more than just work! Of course, he knew his fantasies would run rampant all week now. He'd have to coach himself: take it slow, brother, take it slow.

He distracted himself by making some food from Jackie's list, *Totally Easy Tortellini,* and heating up his leftover chicken.

Chapter Eight

†

Ruthie woke up early Friday morning to the sound of wind whistling through the cottonwoods and the shutters banging noisily from the porch of her friend's cabin. She had meant to find some sort of latch to close the shutters, but she was lucky just to be able to take care of the basics in the old place which, even in its heyday, probably had no particular charm. Although it had a view of the Sauk River, it was a simple cabin with a room or two that had been added later. It always had something that needed fixing, and she still had to fill the back of the toilet with a hose in order to get it to flush.

Garret didn't seem like the rustic type, she reflected, as she went about her morning chores. From the little store in Marblemount she bought fresh halibut, a bottle of white wine, and some fresh coffee for the morning. She'd even splurged on some bear claws and made a big batch of pasta salad. And she decided to dig out some good CDs. After all, he was a great dance partner.

She thought about the way his hand had grasped her waist in dance class—loosely but urgently, a touch that was subtle, pulsing with the downbeats of the song. Even when their feet were doing something intricate, his hands had let her know which direction they were headed. And he had said he couldn't dance. She wasn't buying it. His instincts were right in there.

The next morning, the wind still rattled the shutters. She gathered kindling from the woodpile outside, and on her way inside she heard someone leaving a message on the answering machine. Fioretti. She stopped for a second and listened as he said that he was finishing up his Vancouver, B.C. project and wanted to stop by on his way down to Seattle. She set down the load of loose sticks and wood scraps. Well, she didn't have time to talk now anyway.

She made a pot of coffee and filled a thermos, adding it to the granola bars and water in her backpack, next to the extra rain ponchos. The river would be rough. She tried to keep her mind on what she was doing, but it wasn't easy. She hadn't expected to hear from Fioretti for a few more days and wasn't in the mood for anything complicated.

Things had been left unresolved between them, to say the least. After the dinner at Wild Ginger, she'd given him a ride to his parents' house. She was rather surprised to find both his parents there, but they were cordial in a non-intrusive sort of way and his father even joked about what a Don Juan Fioretti tried to be back in high school.

Fioretti invited her into the small apartment he was staying in downstairs and started putting some moves on her.

"Part of me really wants this," she'd said, and he answered quickly, "Well, *all* of me does." Whatever had changed about him, she'd thought, it wasn't his limited grasp of nuance. But there hadn't been anything really wrong with where they were and what they were doing. Even the fact that his parents were right upstairs hadn't really bothered her, not after all the time that had passed.

But something else distracted her. She didn't know that night if it was something about Fioretti specifically, or something else entirely, but something felt urgent, like a foghorn blast from a ferry in a thick storm. But thinking back, she realized even that night that despite his apparent worldliness, she felt as if she had outgrown him. She told him she had to leave, that she had to get up early the next morning. He said he understood, and she didn't stop to see if he meant it.

On Friday morning, Garret parked near the Monorail Espresso with the outdoor walk-up window. As soon as he got out of his car, his face was saturated with the moisture of a mild morning drizzle. He lined up under an awning behind a couple of business types and started looking for Diane.

"Hey Garret!"

He turned around and there was Diane in a turquoise Gore-Tex rain suit and colorful knit tam pulled down over her blonde hair.

"Diane, it's good to see you. And how about your mom? Is she joining us?"

Diane shook her head. "My aunt arrived yesterday and the two of them decided to stay in town."

Garret tried to hide his disappointment. "So. What are you having?"

"Oh, a single tall, non-fat latte. Thanks."

As they climbed into his car he remembered he had meant to replace the wipers. The rain didn't look like it was going to let up. "Looks like you came prepared for the weather."

"I splurged this week," she admitted, clicking her seatbelt in place. "It's been so long since I've bought any clothes that I made a special trip to REI and a few other places."

"How did everything else go for you this week?"

"Not bad, actually. Dan's been out of town on business, so I spent lots of time with Mom. Things have been chaotic at school, after this Columbine incident, but I've got a good sub covering for me today. A lot of parents are asking for tighter security, but some other ones are questioning the policies about searching backpacks for weapons."

"I can imagine," Garret said, remembering the interviews he'd watched amidst all the chaos.

While they were making their way slowly to the freeway, he wiped the inside of the windshield with a towel. The morning jazz show was just starting.

"Say, I think I found a good divorce lawyer," Diane said. "One of the people on that list you gave me. And I met with my dad's life insurance agent." She started to chuckle. "He had more life insurance than anybody thought, and it all goes to my mom, my brother, and me."

"Do you think your husband knew about the insurance?"

"Well, he never mentioned it, that's for sure." There was a certain satisfaction in her voice.

"How's your mom doing?"

"She still seems pretty numb. She's not saying much, and her doctor gave her sedatives to help her get to sleep. But she seemed genuinely happy to have her sister visiting."

He turned up the fan to try and get the defrost to work better. "It's too bad about the storm. Ruth said she wanted to take us out on a raft to show us some of the eagle sanctuary from the water, but it might be too wet and windy."

"Yeah? My dad was always very gung-ho about the eagles, and how we had that one nest on the property. I've been thinking that maybe if Dan had spent more time up there, hiking around or rafting, or just camping out, maybe he would have gotten the point a little more. It's partly my fault, not going out there more just to have fun together. It seems like every time we went out we had some chore to do. To him, it was just an investment."

Her voice sounded more reflective now, without some of the bitterness he'd heard earlier in the week. The almost matter-of-fact voice of Billie Holiday coming through the speakers seemed to mellow whatever remaining tension there might have been.

"You know, we've been married twelve years. It's very peculiar how there are all these distractions in a marriage. The amount of time you invest in your spouse—it adds up. The accommodations you make, the times you think 'I'll put my idea on the back burner and see what *he* wants to do.' You always think that, somehow, things are going to materialize, things are going to start to build. But instead of some kind of foundation taking shape, now it feels like we were just on a treadmill."

"Did you want to have children?"

"That's been a big problem. We've been trying but nothing's worked. Dan kept saying I was probably infertile, but when we went to a clinic it turned out it was him. Low sperm count. He's had some odd reactions to the whole thing." She seemed to choose her words carefully. "Sometimes he acts like it's this huge metaphor for our relationship, and then other times he acts nonchalant, like maybe he's going through the motions for my benefit and he's lukewarm about having kids."

Garret wasn't quite sure how to respond but he felt relieved that she was willing to level with him. "Well, it's a pretty delicate situation for any guy."

As they left the freeway and headed toward Arlington, the heavy rain turned to a slight mist and he slowed down the wipers. Some of the clouds seemed to be separating.

"You know, my dad was very taken with Ruth."

"Well, she's an intriguing person. And she and your dad seemed to get along well."

"He told me she counted eagles up there every Wednesday during the winter season."

"I think Ruthie felt very cut off toward the end. She had a lot of unresolved feelings when he passed. She and your dad used to talk on the phone a lot, until Dan put a stop to it."

"He what?"

Garret was surprised that Diane seemed shocked. "Yeah. You didn't know? Your dad said he'd have Dan look over the agreements before transferring the land over to the Conservancy. But a couple weeks after that, Dan sent a fax to Ruthie and me saying we should both stop talking to Arnie, 'cause his illness was progressing."

He glanced over at Diane, and she had her arms crossed tightly against her chest. She grimaced.

"I've never run into anything that formal except from somebody who was planning a lawsuit," he added. "So, we stopped calling your father and waited for some kind of move from Dan. The only person we were authorized to talk to was your father's CPA, and he never got back to us."

"I don't understand Dan. This is exactly the kind of thing I was talking about. As if he can control your free speech." Her voice sounded sharp. "I detest that. I believe in the Bill of Rights—old-fashioned, I guess. I mean, you're adults. So you call Arnie, and maybe my mother tells you he's taking a nap or not feeling well. Fine. That would be up to my parents, not Dan."

Garret guided the car around a series of curves and turned down the fan and the car radio; the station had become mostly static.

"The more I hear about this relationship you and Ruth had with Dan, the more I'm convinced he's gone off the deep end. And you were the one who sent those John Coltrane CDs, right? My father loved those. You know ... my dad's relationship with the Conservancy went back quite a few years. Before he got sick, he used to like to go up to the river a lot, even if he had to go alone. He said his dream was to be able to volunteer on the eagle inventories."

"Yup, he told Ruthie that. She told him not to feel bad about not being able to do more up there himself. She said that the donation he was making was important to those eagles—and salmon and the whole cycle of life up there, including people."

"She sounds like quite a lady." He thought Diane might sound resentful, but she didn't. "You know, in my case, since Dad got sick, I was grateful when people took an interest in him, especially somebody who understood the importance of his land. Dan took his role way too seriously. If anyone had the right to try and manage that relationship, it should have been my mother, or possibly me, if she wasn't up to it."

They rode quietly as they got closer to the property. Ruthie *was* quite a lady, Garret thought as he drove, passing White Horse Mountain again, the cottonwoods along the rushing river, coming closer to the Cascades, the mountains that made Ruthie feel like life was grandiose and beautiful. Seeing the mountains again was just as dramatic as the first time—even in the fog.

When he had first met Ruthie with Arnie, she was working. Negotiating, actually. He knew now that she had a subtle touch, a certain easy way with people. But he hadn't really started to notice her subtleties until the dance class. He'd learned to hold back, guard himself. He had almost become a master of it. After all, he was still recovering from Jackie and he didn't want anyone breaking his shield, his great excuse to block his feelings. The trouble was, he was blocking them even from himself. And Ruthie wasn't just *anyone*.

In college, he'd told himself that he would only marry a black woman. Not that he'd dwelled on the idea, or even talked much about it with his friends, but he'd wanted to nurture his African blood, not dilute it. He told his dad once, and his dad had nodded, agreeing that it made sense in theory. "But things don't always work out the way you plan, son," his dad added. "Sometimes you have to see where the Most High is going to guide you, 'cause the woman you end up with is going to be the one you can work it out with spiritually. You may not have society on your side, but if you've got that spiritual bond, you can make it."

When he was dancing with Ruthie at that class, the combination of ethnicities she represented had crossed his mind. Her grandparents on one side were Romani—people from India, the Middle East, the Mediterranean, and North Africa, many of whom had intermarried with African slaves. She couldn't be labeled any more than he could. Racial classifications were absurd, for sure.

The private road into the McGowans' place was muddier than before, with puddles between sections of gravel that splashed up against the car. He noticed the big yellow gate was open as he pulled into the short driveway. That was odd, but they continued on up past the metal shed and parked.

"Well, here we are," Diane said. They walked over to the cabin and Garret stretched as Diane unlocked the door.

Stepping inside, Garret turned slowly, his eyes scanning the dimly lit room. The place was full of stuff—clothes, an open sleeping bag, food, and dishes. Stuff that Garret knew had definitely not been there before. He turned to Diane, who was looking around with an expression of mild confusion.

"This is really bizarre," he told her. "When I was up here with Ruthie a few weeks ago, this place was almost empty. Are you sure your mom didn't send someone up here in her place? Or maybe hire a caretaker?"

"No! I would have known. I didn't know there was anybody staying here!"

Garret gave her a look, but she didn't notice. She walked toward a pile of boxes in the corner. As he followed behind her, he could see that they held magazines and stacks of paper. Diane stooped down and starting pulling out a few envelopes.

"Garret?" she said, her voice muffled as she shuffled through the boxes.

But Garret was distracted. He was looking past her, into one of the boxes. Stacked inside were dozens of typed pages. Newsletters. He recognized the banner of the Caucasian Nations.

"Oh shit," she said. "This is Dan's mail." She held it out toward Garret, her brow wrinkled in confusion.

"Diane—I think we should—" He started to help her up.

Suddenly, the door to the cabin was shoved open from the outside. A tall blondish guy carrying a rifle stepped noisily into the room.

"What do you mean, 'oh shit?'" he said, glaring past Garret at Diane. "I thought by now you'd be over our little tiff."

"You can put the gun down, Dan. We're not some thieves barging in." Her voice sounded deliberately gentle, almost condescending, as if speaking to one of her students to get them to settle down.

"You can relax, and I'll put the gun down when I'm good and ready. In fact, you two can sit down at that nice picnic table there and keep yourselves calm."

Garret straightened up and moved closer to Diane. "Look, I got nothing to be nervous about," Garret told him.

"That's the spirit. But like I said," he moved further into the room, "I need you two sitting right here at this picnic table. And I don't need you messing around in my mail."

Dan looked larger, more muscular and fit than the low-energy lawyer Garret had pictured sitting at his desk with his feet up, occasionally taking phone calls, maybe looking into a case or two if he felt like it.

They sat down slowly on the bench, their legs facing outwardly and their backs against the table. Diane folded her arms, dropping her head. Dan had his gun pointed in the air, away from them, but it was hanging precariously from a shoulder strap.

"So what's with all the hate literature, Gibbs?" Garret asked, trying to sound nonchalant as he made more room for Diane on the bench.

"Caucasian Nations? They're not a hate group. They just say people need to separate so they can live in some kind of peace, that's all. Live with people who understand them. They're people who are sick and tired of being abused and misunderstood." Dan spoke with a confidence Garret hadn't heard on the phone.

"Well, they ought to try someplace like Antarctica," Garret said, trying to think of somewhere far away."

"Look, asshole," Dan walked over to their bench, resting the butt of the rifle on his boot. "I don't know who the hell you are, okay? And I'll tell you what. I don't give a rat's ass. You drive around the state with my goddamn wife, then I know all I need to know about you. You better account for yourself, you punk." He glared at Garret, daring him to answer.

"Dan, you have got to be kidding." Diane looked up at him, her face a mix of fear, confusion, and shock. "He's the bank trust officer. He brought me up here to meet with the conservation staff." She folded her arms more tightly across her chest and shot him a defiant look. "This property belongs to my mom and you have no right to be on it."

"Sorry, honey," Dan said in a mocking tone. His eyes lingered for a moment more on Garret, before he finally shifted his gaze back to Diane. "I'm the executor of her estate, along with your dumb ass, so I've got all the authority I need to be on it."

"This is such bullshit," she muttered.

"Why don't you shut the fuck up? I've had enough of your self-righteous elitist crap," he hollered.

He held onto the gun, tipping it so that it pointed towards them as he went over and locked the door. Then he grabbed a stool from the corner and plopped it down roughly in front of them. He shifted the gun casually as he sat down.

Garret's mind began to race. He could feel chemicals rushing into his brain like poison, and his body felt like a pile of rocks. This was a stone set-up. It had to be. And he'd fallen for it hook, line, and sinker.

"So where do you come from, Carter?" Dan asked him, using the same smug tone as their first phone conversation.

"Chicago." He spoke without emotion. How could he have fallen for Diane's act? All that grief over her father? Garret felt like kicking himself for not looking into Diane's story more. But why him? What was his presence adding to whatever scheme these guys had going on?

"So your folks are black, or one of 'em is?"

"Look, what difference does that make? If I'm black, does that make me dangerous? Is that why you think you need that gun? You think I might suddenly jump up and slit your throat with a straight razor? Man, you been watching too many movies."

Dan gave him a stone-faced look.

Garret tried to moderate his anger, convert venting into something that might actually make sense. "Maybe it means I'm not as sharp as you? Or not as cagey? If I'm black, does it mean you're a better lawyer than I am? Or that when you wake up in the morning you have more energy than I do, more enthusiasm for the day, more ability to get things done? So that no matter what I do right this minute, you're always going to be one step ahead of me?"

Garret watched him shift his weight on the stool before he answered, his eyes narrowing as he focused.

"Look, prob'ly none of that." He kept the rifle butt on his boot. "I'm just up to here with all the P.C. bullshit. Go ahead—take out my fucking wife, I don't care. I'm off the hook now anyway. I'm in the process of divesting myself from the McGowan clan—with pleasure."

"Good," Diane added, her voice sharp. Garret glanced at her, trying to gauge her sincerity.

"Look—I've heard enough out of you. If you're not going to help out, then shut the fuck up. And you, too, buster. I don't need you two wrecking my plans. What the hell's in that backpack? Go get it. And no bull shitting around with me."

Diane grabbed her pack near the door.

"Empty it over here," he said. There was a water bottle, a flashlight, some power bars, and a phone.

"Give me that phone." Dan threw it into a bucket and poured the water from the water bottle over it. "You don't get that one phone call in this joint, honey. That reminds me."

He kicked the cabin land phone across the floor, sat back down on the stool, set it on his knee and punched in some numbers. "Abbot. You gotta get out here pronto. I've got visitors." He paused, listening into the phone. "I ain't lying. Get your butt out here, and bring some rags and some rope." He hung up the phone.

Noticing Garret's interest in the phone, he gave him a tight, menacing smile and stuck it under his stool.

Still holding the rifle, he managed to pull out a thin cigar about the size of a cigarette and light it with a pocket lighter. "This deal is going to be so clean, no one will even know it went down. Like I said, once it's done, I'm going to be able to extricate myself from all this McGowan family bullshit and get on with my life. Maybe move to Idaho with some like-minded folk."

"Heaven forbid," said Diane under her breath, perhaps for Garret's benefit.

Garret hadn't mentioned Dan's earlier Caucasian Nations remark to her, a definite screw-up on his part, he realized now. If she was on the level, and she wasn't part of this scheme, whatever it was, then she might have been able to connect the dots before they'd even headed out here. And if she'd been in on it from the start, his bringing it up might have gotten her to let the cat out of the bag. But Garret really had no clue. The whole thing was swirling around him like little bombs going off in the astral plane.

He tried to slow down his breathing, trying to create some sense of space and time. The air in the room felt thick around him, heavy; he felt paralyzed, almost like he was encased in a pool of invisible jello. He felt that if he tried to move, it would be in slow motion. Frustrated, he chided himself—he had been too eager to come up and see Ruthie, used the excuse of bringing Diane up to visit the property so that he could see her. He had let himself get distracted, that was his first mistake. And he'd been too trusting. He should have had Diane checked out some way. And Gibbs—he'd known he was questionable from the start. In fact, this entire donation had been full of red flags, with Dan giving out the most resounding warning signs. No rules in his law books informed Garret about how to deal with a character like this one.

And the damn yellow gate, Garret thought angrily. It had been wide open! How could he have been so lame?

On the stool in front of him, Dan puffed his cigar smugly, shortening the shoulder strap of his rifle and raising the butt of the gun to his hip, his hand near the trigger, staring all the while at them. Satisfied that he had control. The smoke was making Garret nauseous.

Only Garret's part-time life on the streets as a teenage wanna-be acting fearless gave him an inkling about a character like this—a character ruled by self-interest, justifying anything. But even on the streets, there was a code of loyalty, certain people you wouldn't snitch on, people you'd back up in a confrontation no matter what, people you could trust. This guy seemed to be out for stakes that Garret couldn't fathom. He rested his head on his hands.

"See, you two don't recognize the wisdom behind my not telling you what's going down. You know, Diane, you never gave me credit for any kind of honor. Oh no. You reserved your respect for your father, your coworkers, or for some high school principal just because he wasn't banging his students, as far as you could tell. But I have honor," Dan said. Garret looked up for a moment, wondering how much of this was just more mockery. "Yeah, I'm honorable. See, the way I set this up, if something goes down, you'll never be implicated."

The rain outside had picked up. Garret adjusted his back just a bit, rubbing it slightly against the picnic table to ease the stiffness. The raindrops hit the roof loudly like somebody dropping nails on metal, drowning out the sound of his breathing and even the occasional movements of Gibbs' feet. But Garret's mind still ran in circles, a broken record replaying the crap. He leaned forward, dropped his head a little and shifted his weight, feeling sore.

If it weren't for Jackie messing up, falling for some other dude, he wouldn't be here now. That was the biggest irony of all. Here he was, moving to Seattle, trying to get free of the past, and some dude pulls a rifle on him in a cabin in the middle of nowhere. A heck of a way to get free, sitting here five feet from the barrel of a gun.

He closed his eyes, just for a second, the darkness offering a hint of relief. He could feel Diane shifting next to him on the bench. He recalled the words of a poem his father used to quote: 'Out of the night that covers me black as the pit from pole to pole, I thank whatever gods may be for my unconquerable soul.' William Ernst Henley, *Invictus.* He wished he could remember more of it, but his mind had always drifted when his father had recited it and tuned him out.

Sitting on the bench, a hostage, Garret realized he could have listened more. His father had never rejected him when he messed up, even when he was running the streets. Most parents would have blown the whistle on his herb runnings and the booze and his attitude. But his dad—his dad always said he didn't trust the system, and he wasn't about to turn him over. When the chips were down, his father had told him that all he could do was love him. But Garret had barely heard him back then.

It was the same with his mother, he thought, pressing his eyelids together, trying to steady his breathing, trying to ignore the redneck sitting five feet away from him. In high school, their relationship had become pared down to basics, his GPA, his college applications, his test scores. She made sure he didn't let any of that slide. But before that, they'd been close. Camping with him and his brother, telling stories. She would love seeing this place on the river. She'd found ways to get them out of the city, dragging them up to the north woods of Wisconsin every August, sometimes almost obsessively. She'd given him a respect for nature, for beautiful undisturbed places, a respect that made him receptive to someone like Ruthie. And she had a naturalness that defied race.

Dan adjusted his position, scraping the metal legs of his stool against the hard floor, making them screech.

He'd been critical of his parents when he left for college, carrying some kind of unnamed grudge. Grudges about little things: the old car they drove, the old house that needed repairs, the junk they'd accumulated in it. But as he'd grown up and seen what some people had to go through, some with no real safety net from parents at all, he had started seeing his parents in a different light. Through years of feeling restricted and suppressed, his father had managed to hold onto his soul. He'd known it was more important than money. Garret hadn't given his dad credit for it at first, but deep down he knew that the only thing really worth changing your life over was your soul. His dad had taught him that.

Every August his mother went to northern Wisconsin away from the hot humidity of Chicago. She'd tell herself that it was all right his father couldn't leave the city, or wouldn't leave the city, that he liked freedom from pressure. She said she didn't mind sleeping in that cabin room with the mosquitoes buzzing around the single light bulb on the ceiling. She said the place renewed her.

And Garret didn't want to get shot up here, in such a senseless fashion, and who would even know enough to call his parents? And how could he just disappear and not say he understood, that he accepted them for who they were even though they were different from each other, and he didn't mean to call himself a mutt that one summer in her kitchen, when she was packing to go up north and instead of going along he said he was moving out of their house and wouldn't say where to. And he could picture her, slowly walking up that slightly steep path at the lake with those thin wet thongs, up gravel that sometimes slid under your feet, and she might remember when he and his brother were young, swimming in that lake, and in the water time didn't matter and you could say whatever you wanted, and she said she liked to hear the water lapping against the side of the dock, that it was the most peaceful feeling in the world and she never wanted to forget that feeling and she said she knew they would be all right.

Diane sneezed, and it startled him.

"You're messing with God's country," Garret said under his breath.

"What are you mumbling about now, you wuss?"

"This place was supposed to be part of the eagle sanctuary and a big old growth forest project."

"Oh why don't you grow up? So you've aligned yourself with a bunch of tree huggers this week. Who's it going to be next week, some gay rights group? That's what I can't stand about you bleeding hearts—jumping from one cause to another like it's a friggin' shopping mall. You're a bunch of vultures. Get your own goddamn life."

Diane sighed. "How did you become so confused? And so hostile?"

"I told you, I don't need any more of your bullshit questions." He slammed the butt of the rifle against the floor for effect.

Garret leaned over and his calculator fell out of his shirt pocket onto the floor.

"What's this?" Dan's eyes darted to the floor at the sound and he squinted suspiciously at the calculator.

As he leaned down to get it, Garret saw his chance. He slid his leg under Dan's stool, jerking it back so quickly that Dan slid off the stool as it fell, hitting his elbow on the floor and losing control of the rifle just long enough for Garret to grab it.

Garret steadied himself with his legs against the bench and faced Dan, who was struggling to right himself.

"Stand over in the corner and put your hands up. Now!" he said firmly, gesturing with the barrel of the gun. "See, that's the trouble with guns. You never know who might get hold of one." He kept his eyes on Dan's hands as he groped around and slowly stood up. "And put out that cigar!"

"Shit," Dan muttered, smashing the cigar under his foot.

"Gibbs, now you just stay where you are." He glanced back quickly toward the bench, where Diane was staring at the two of them in confusion. "Diane," he said as calmly as he could, "you need to call Ruthie. And tell her to bring the cops. It's on the first page of this notebook." He took the tiny spiral notebook out of his pocket and tossed it over to her.

Diane moved in slow motion, rigidly. The three of them stood there, locked in place, while she dialed.

"I'm just getting an answering machine," she said abruptly.

"That's okay. Leave a message and then call the operator and ask for the police."

"Oh, that's cute." Dan laughed. "Who are you going to call? The county sheriff? He might make it by next week."

Garret didn't answer and kept the gun pointed at him.

"I've got the police station in Concrete," she said after a few moments.

"Good." Garret glanced over at her. "Tell 'em we've got a guy threatening people with a loaded gun, a room full of hate literature, and some kind of deal going down that needs investigating."

"Look, save your breath." Dan sounded calm. Too calm, Garret thought. "You're not going to get any cops up here for hours. Hate literature? Please. My guy'll be here any minute. You let him do what he's s'pose to, and he'll be outta your hair. You don't even need to know about it."

"Okay, Gibbs, it's your turn to relax. You've already implicated Diane's mother with this deal you're trying to pull off, whatever it is, and you've got enough hate literature in here to brainwash half the coast. It's people like you who have made hate crimes across this country a reality. How are people supposed to recover from crap like that? If you want to start a revolution, go ahead, but out and out hate? Racism? Please." He shook his head. "Talk about bullshit—that's four-star."

Dan grimaced. "You wouldn't understand. People just want to be left alone. The race issue—it's not racism. It's not hate, it's pride. It's a form of bonding."

Garret laughed freely. "Oh that's rich. Yeah, the next time my buddy and I get pulled over by a couple of cops and they don't give us any reason, I won't worry about it. I'll just tell 'em, 'Oh, that's okay, I know you all are just bonding. You're just carryin' the white man's burden.'" Garret laughed again. This guy was unreal.

Without the gun, Dan had no backbone. But Garret wasn't really buying his nonchalant manner; he wasn't going to bank on anything at this juncture. He looked around the room for rope—something to make Dan, and the situation, a little more secure—but there was nothing in sight. The damn rifle was heavy, too, heavier than a tenor sax. He'd held a rifle a few times at a summer camp, but this was not his usual pastime. What he was supposed to be good at was keeping his cool, and he'd done a pretty good job at it until this joker came along.

The best strategy now was to keep Dan at a distance, 'cause things could get ugly in no time if he got too close. While pretending to be nonchalant, Dan was studying his every move. Diane moved another stool close to the door and held on to the phone. Garret could only pray that she'd really dialed those numbers and actually talked to the cops. After all, these two were still married. Weirder things had gone down.

Looking at the two of them, Garret thought of the crazies who used to come into the post office when his dad was working the front counter. Usually his dad had kept it cool and even talked people down. But once, he got his hand shot, and another time he started going off at some comment about his dreadlocks. He'd come to the end of his rope. He was taken off the front counter then, and he hadn't fought it, taking a job sorting stuff in the back.

Garret wondered if this was going to be the moment he finally lost *his* cool. He kept the gun pointed on Dan and took a long breath.

Ruthie dropped the raft off at the put-in on forest service land and took her car down to Marblemount, where Rob from State Parks gave her a ride back to the raft. He was skeptical about her going out alone in this weather, but she insisted she'd be fine. She told him she was only going two miles by herself, that she'd be picking people up at the McGowan place.

"I tell you what," Rob said, trying to offer her a compromise. "My tour group's not coming for a couple more hours. I could join you on the float. This wind is getting rough—any more than this and we'll have to start canceling trips."

Ruthie thought about it. Rob was a good guy, adventuresome and a great rower, and he had never struck her as one to exaggerate.

"I promise I'll be careful. The only trick will be turning left onto their place early enough that I don't get diverted by the current."

He finally acquiesced, but he gave her an extra paddle.

"Just in case," he said as he handed it to her. "If you do miss your turn-off, just go on down to the park and one of our guys can drive you back."

"Aye-eye, sir." Ruthie saluted. She wasn't worried. She'd been on this river before when it was plenty rough, including a few times during snowstorms. She had plenty of experience, but she wouldn't be taking the group out if this wind didn't ease up.

But Rob had been right about the current. There was very little paddling to do; the water pulled her forward aggressively. The raft surged ahead, going twice as fast as normal, and she had to stay clear of the center just to maintain some control. Using her paddle as a rudder, she managed to slow herself down. It was so dark the water looked black.

At this speed, the raft chopped against the water, almost like a motorboat, and suddenly she was on top of a log. She tried to gently pry herself loose, but the current kept slapping her up against it. She knew it might have sharp branches that could poke through the raft. She tried shoving herself off with the paddle and bracing herself up, but she still couldn't get loose. Finally, she took off her gloves, stuck her hands in the freezing water, grabbed a branch attached to the log, and raised herself up enough to push free. In the summer this sort of thing was child's play, but now her hands were freezing and she couldn't get her gloves back on.

Because of the current, she was travelling almost sideways.

Holding the rifle at constant eye level was making Garret's arms so sore he almost couldn't feel them; his hands felt hard and stiff where they connected to the gun. Diane sat next to the door, almost motionless with the phone next to her feet. He could insist that she go and get some help, but would she? Gibbs was still pretending to be calm, but his eyes jetted with each sound, darting up as a tree branch brushed against the roof. He was waiting vigilantly for Garret to drop his guard. Garret felt as if the hours were creeping by, or as if time had simply stopped.

They were three statues now, and he was probably the reason they were still alive. Gibbs was a loose cannon; any move Garret made would be risky. Still, the longer he waited, the closer Gibbs' guy got.

"Gibbs, if you move I'm going to shoot your leg off," he said, finally making a decision. He threw his keys to Diane, who finally focused back into attention and clutched them to her chest. "Take my car, go to the ranger station, and tell them to get over here with the sheriff or a cop or somebody. Pronto."

Gibbs chortled loudly in uneven sputters, releasing tension like an engine with a weak battery. Garret dreaded being alone with the guy and he knew he was taking a big chance by trusting Diane again. Who the hell was she really working with? But with Dan's buddy on his way, he had nothing to lose by sending her, and a ton to gain if she was on his side.

Diane looked relieved to have something to do and ran out the door.

He heard the engine turn over and thought he heard Diane backing out away from the cabin. But then he heard another vehicle that rattled like a big truck. It sounded close. He heard a door slam.

"All right, lady. Get out of that car and put your hands up. Now!" said a voice from outside. "That's a good girl." Garret heard something snap. "Get inside that cabin."

And then, suddenly, time sped up again.

Diane threw open the door and rushed into the cabin. The window behind Garret's head shattered. "Drop it!" someone shouted from outside, and shot just above Garret's head.

Before he had a chance to react, the guy from outside rushed in. He burst through the door with a sawed-off shotgun, and threw Gibbs a big revolver. "Drop it, I said!" he screamed as he and Gibbs pointed their weapons at him.

Garret let the rifle drop to the floor.

"Get in the corner, you shit! Over on that bunk!" Gibbs pointed his gun at Garret while the other guy tied his hands behind his back with a rag and then tied him to the bottom bunk with a length of thick rope. Gibbs pointed his gun at Diane. "Her, too." The other guy tied her to the bench of the picnic table and started cutting one of the rags. Gibbs watched impatiently from the doorway. "Gag their mouths, too. I've heard enough from them both. What took you so long?"

"Look, just keep cool. I think my phone's bugged so I took a few detours."

"All the more reason to speed this up. Hand me your keys and I'll go load up. And keep your eye on both of 'em. This bum's been tryin' to get smart with me."

Garret heard the heavy footsteps of Gibbs leaving, and then listened to the sound of the truck turning over. The noise from the engine faded; he seemed to be heading in the direction of the river. Garret's blindfold was so tight his temples throbbed. He heard the guy take a long drink of water, and realized he was thirsty.

"Don't try any funny stuff, asshole. If it was up to me, you guys'd be out of the picture any way this goes down—back off in the woods, being fed to the worms."

On the river, the wind blew thick, horizontal sheets of fog across the water. Ruthie managed to get off the current and slide up next to the bank for a clearer view, but it was no use. She could only see a few feet ahead of her. The water was so dark she couldn't make out rocks or logs until she was almost on top of them. When she came to a shallower stretch where she could recognize the whitish gravel bottom of the river, she tried to slow herself down but the current still kept her going at a fast clip. The fog turned to mist and then to rain. Trying to estimate where she was, she suddenly came to a large crescent-shaped gravel bar that seemed familiar and, scanning the riverbank, recognized the cedar shakes of the McGowans' boathouse.

Gratefully, she slid her raft up onto the gravel and jumped out, surprised that the door to the boathouse was wide open. Dragging the raft well beyond the water line, she noticed new-looking tire tracks along the top of the riverbank. Who would have driven all the way to the boathouse and then left the door open? She followed the thick wet tracks up to where they met with the trail and continued on most of the way to the cabin. Garret's car was parked in the driveway but it was empty, and then she noticed the broken window. What was going on? She waited, listening for sounds, but it was quiet except for the swishing of branches brushing against the roof.

Slowly, she opened the cabin door, which was unlocked, and looked inside. The room looked as if it had been hit by a hurricane, with broken glass scattered all over the floor. A sleeping bag had been thrown carelessly into a corner and the picnic table was covered in piles of mail and papers. She picked a few up and saw that they were flyers and brochures from the Caucasian Nations. The mail had Dan Gibbs' name on it, which gave her the creeps. Under a stack of brochures she noticed an empty box for rifle shells. She picked it up and turned it over. In small letters it read "Property of Ft. Lewis."

Something was horribly wrong. And Garret's car was there but where was Garret?

The cabin phone was torn out of the wall. She tried her cell but she couldn't get a signal. She walked over to Garret's car and peered inside. The keys were still in the ignition, which didn't make sense. Something was definitely wrong.

She drove the abandoned car down the driveway and back out to the highway. She knew there was a phone outside the forest service office. Maybe Garret had called her. Maybe there was an explanation for what she'd found at the McGowan place.

Holding her breath, she punched the number to her friend's cabin and pressed the receiver against her ear. Instead of hearing Garret's voice, she listened with growing disbelief to a garbled message from Diane Gibbs. Her voice was anxious and troubling, telling her to try to get to the police and not to come to the property. She said that Dan had a gun and was trying to pull off some sort of illegal deal.

Ruthie listened to the message again before slowly setting the phone back into its cradle. Had Dan really flipped out? Was he walking around with a loaded weapon? She remembered what Garret had told her he'd said about the Caucasian Nations. "Those guys need rifles, just like anybody else." Her heart was pounding.

She picked the phone back up and called the operator, asked for the police, and was patched through to the police station in Concrete.

"Look lady," the officer on the other end said, after she'd recounted the phone message and mentioned the McGowan property. "We've already sent somebody out there. Sergeants Sanchez and Brown are on their way. Should be there anytime. You're going to need to stay out of there until they can investigate the premises."

Ruthie explained that she'd already been there and described the mess she'd found at the cabin. She told him that she'd found

Garret's car, and borrowed it so she could get to the pay phone. She explained to them that the situation was urgent—that Garret Carter and Diane Gibbs were missing. The cop told her to come into the station and file a report.

Chapter Nine

†

Garret was sprawled along the side of the van, having been thrown in on his side by Gibbs. His hands were still tied behind his back, and even his feet were bound together now. He was blindfolded. His clothes were wet. His body was heavy against cardboard boxes filled with contents that rattled loudly over the rough traction of the van. Diane coughed next to him, the sound muffled by a rag around her mouth. He heard Gibbs say something from the front seat but couldn't make out the words. The rag that was forcing his jaw open chafed against his lips. He could barely swallow, and for a minute he started to choke on his own saliva.

The boxes beneath him gave a loud metallic clang with Gibbs's words about the Caucasian Nations reverberating. "They need rifles, just like anybody else." He could tell this Abbot character, with the sawed off shotgun, was totally into weapons, too. These had to be boxes full of guns. And given the turn of events, transporting them, maybe even selling them, had to be the big deal Gibbs was talking about pulling off. These guys are off the deep-end, Garret thought, shifting against the boxes. Far enough gone that they could dump his body anywhere. His ears popped. He figured they must be gaining elevation, heading toward the Cascades. He could be dropped off the edge of a cliff somewhere in the mountains and never heard from again.

Here he'd thought he'd achieved some sense of worldliness, getting offered the job in Seattle. But his father had warned him. He said you could never predict what might happen in Babylon. He hadn't predicted *this*.

Garret's parents had helped him move out of his Chicago apartment. They'd spent two days moving boxes and half a night re-packing stuff into mailing crates, cutting duct tape like it was going out of style. But the day he was set to leave he woke up feeling ready. His dad was an early riser and had made some oatmeal by 6:00. Garret said goodbye to his mom, who was still sleepy, and then he and his pops headed to the airport. Garret felt excited, just like he had when he first left for college. After all, it was his first job out of Chicago and he had been recruited for it. He told his dad that while the black population wasn't all that large in Seattle, it was pretty vocal, and that there had even been a black mayor the year before.

"Well, son, I don't know what you can conclude from that, given the nature of politicians. My suggestion would be that you take it a little slow deciding who you can trust."

Garret felt bruised all along the side of his body from being forced into the vehicle and landing hard on his right side. But with his hands tied behind him, trying to shift to his back to relieve some of his soreness was impossible. He could hear Abbot and Gibbs arguing in the front seat, something about using the phone, but the rattling of the boxes beneath him drowned most of it out. They seemed to be moving at a faster clip than before. He was too thirsty now to be hungry, and weak enough that he had to focus all his energy on staying alert.

His father had been right, and Garret had been too trusting. He'd ignored the red flags and followed this case right into a trap. But it was his life and it mattered: attachments to people, to family, to places, even to ideas. The weirder these two guys in the front seat got with their arguing, their speculations about the tapped phone, the clanging of metal in boxes beneath him, the more he realized he had a strong sense of justice. This predicament with Gibbs was pulling his coat.

Ruthie sat in the Concrete police station's waiting room. A tall bald guy with a big stomach came out of the glass-enclosed office in front, where somebody named Sergeant Olson was on the phone.

"Look Miss Adams, I'm sorry you had to wait so long. I'm Detective Jenkins," he said as they shook hands. "You look like you got pretty wet out there."

"It's all right. I've been sitting here next to the radiator and drying out."

"If you don't mind, maybe we could step into the office in the back."

She followed the detective into a very small windowless room that had nothing but a metal desk and two folding chairs inside. He seemed too large for the room, for the small metal chair and the thin clipboard balanced on his lap.

"So. Sergeant Sanchez called in this missing persons report. What about this guy Dan Gibbs? Ever met him?"

She shook her head no.

"So, we have no information on this guy except for the phone call that came in from his wife, saying that he was brandishing a weapon on this property near Marblemount. Is there anything you can tell us that might corroborate what his wife was saying? Is it possible this was just some sort of domestic dispute?"

"That could be folded into it, but it seems like more than that. When Garret Carter was in our office in Mount Vernon, Dan Gibbs told him that he had sympathies for the Caucasian Nations. He said, 'They need rifles, just like anybody else.'"

"And did Mr. Carter report this behavior at all?"

"Not that I know of. I can't speak for him, but I believe he took it more as a provocative remark, rather than something Gibbs was acting on."

"So he didn't take it completely seriously—as far as you know."

"I think he took it seriously, but maybe not literally," Ruthie answered, a little impatiently. Why was this guy focusing on Garret when there was clear evidence that Gibbs was dangerous?

"Look, Miss Adams," the detective said, sensing her frustration. "I'm not trying to put you on the defensive. I'm just trying not to draw any conclusions yet."

"I understand that. I don't know your field but I would expect that criminology is a science like any other." She took a deep breath, feeling her normally long fuse get shorter and shorter. "Like conservation science, for instance. When I'm monitoring the impacts of a prescribed burn, I have to inventory all the species—all the plants, insects, migratory activity, every type of life I can find. I may have a theory about native plant recovery, but if I see invasives, then I have to report that." As she was speaking, she noticed the detective was paying less and less attention. She felt like saying she was trying to save the damn planet and wasn't he supposed to be saving people from harm, so what was the real difference anyway? She cleared her throat. "I don't see how the evidence you collect would be that different."

"Well thank you for that little introduction to the work you do." He gave her a slightly bored look. "So, if you believe that I'm overlooking some important evidence, by all means, enlighten me, Miss Adams."

In fact, Ruthie did believe he was overlooking important evidence. "What about the hate literature?" she asked him, trying to keep her voice level.

"The last time I looked at the Bill of Rights, you could still collect any kind of printed material you want. Maybe Gibbs was studying it."

"Studying it? If that's the case, why would he need so many copies of one brochure? I think it's more likely he was trying to disseminate it. Plus what about the shell box?"

"Oh, that ammo box with a possible connection to Fort Lewis? If Gibbs is former military, he could have saved some shell boxes. Not all that incriminating."

A *possible* connection? Ruthie shook her head. She couldn't believe the guy was acting so blasé.

"Look Miss Adams. We've got these officers out there at the crime scene still searching the place, looking for neighbors to interview, pretty much combing the entire vicinity. I'm not sure what else we can do right now." He looked back down at his notes and told her she could leave. Was this the usual approach for folks in the back country? He hardly seemed curious. Did he think that threatening people with loaded weapons was a standard MO? Maybe she had left out some important detail.

As Jenkins walked out of the room, she heard Olson tell him that somebody from ATF was on the phone for him. Ruthie went over to the water cooler in the waiting room and took as long as possible getting herself a drink. Finally, the detective walked back out of the glass office.

"Ah, Miss Adams, we got a call from Alcohol, Tobacco, and Firearms. It's very preliminary, but there seems to be a stockpile of weapons missing from Ft. Lewis near Tacoma. So, thanks to your detective work, we may have a possible link with this Gibbs guy. And I do mean possible. ATF is doing a search out there by the base and their security is on alert."

"Are you saying that Gibbs might have stolen weapons from Ft. Lewis?"

"Possibly. It's too soon to say. But from Diane Gibbs' call to this office, it seems possible Gibbs was talking about a weapons deal. We don't know for sure exactly what's missing. If I were you, I would steer clear of that McGowan property, and don't go near Gibbs' house or his office. We'll notify you if we learn anything more." He reached into his pocket and pulled out a business card. "Here's my card. Give me a call if you hear anything."

So that was it. One tiny little baby step at a time. "Well, what about my friend—my colleague, I mean, Mr. Carter? Will you be looking for him? And Diane Gibbs?" She suddenly felt a chill. Was this guy even taking this case seriously? If he didn't, then who would?

"Look, lady, we're doing everything we can. None of this is easy. I suggest you find a safe place and, like I said, call us if you learn anything else."

When the van stopped again, Garret could hear the loud mechanical vibration of trucks nearby. The smell of fuel and oil and rubber was overpowering. It had to be a gas station.

Abbot said something he couldn't make out. He heard the door slam and Gibbs' voice from up front telling him and Diane not to move, and another series of metallic sounds as Abbot started filling the tank. The door slammed again—Abbot climbing back inside—and then Gibbs said he had to take a leak. Garret was dying to take a piss, too, but that wasn't about to happen.

Garret realized this was the first time in his life that he wished the cops would stop the vehicle he was in for any reason at all. Broken tail light. Going a few miles over the limit. Anything. Had these guys thought of everything? Like tinted windows, for instance? Garret had to stay still just to keep from pissing on himself, but he knew he was lucky just to be alive.

Back on the road, he felt them climbing again for awhile, and then suddenly they started dropping altitude. Fast. Gibbs yelled at Abbot to slow down, and Garret thought he mumbled something about ice. He felt them skid in a few places, the vehicle losing traction. They started to climb again, and then Garret was rocked from side to side as the truck zigzagged. They took a hard turn, Garret's body sliding a few inches on cardboard, and he heard Gibbs tell Abbot he thought they were on the wrong road. The van slowed, idled for a few minutes, and he listened to Diane's muffled whimpers. Then they lurched forward and swung around. Garret's temples were still throbbing, and now he felt nauseous from all the twisting and turning.

He tried to transport himself somewhere else, tried to imagine what Ruthie's cabin on the Sauk River looked like. He imagined having dinner with her, maybe spending the night, and going to the park that she had raved about, the one with the very old trees. He visualized a little section of woods, where it was mossy—warm and moist and comfortable—and he could lie next to her on the soft ground and the two of them… it would be like going back to nature. That was how he felt about Ruthie, completely uninhibited, if she would have him. He wondered where she was now, glad that she hadn't walked into the trap the way he had. That, at least, was a blessing.

Ruthie drove Garret's car back toward her cabin. Who else could she call to help out? She knew she should call Rob and let him know she was safely off the river, but could she possibly begin to describe what was happening?

When she pulled up, a familiar black Mustang was parked in the driveway. "You've got to be kidding me," she mumbled, and climbed out of the car. "Fioretti, what are you doing here?"

"Merda. I didn't realize you'd be so glad to see me." He looked as if he'd been standing on the porch waiting.

"I'm sorry." She shook her head as if to clear it. "I forgot I gave you the directions out here."

"Ruthie, are you okay? You look tense." He started toward her but she fumbled with the door locks on Garret's car.

"I'm *not* okay." She didn't elaborate. "Well, since you're here," she said stiffly, gesturing at the door.

Fioretti followed her inside and waited as she took off her damp vest and jacket. "I hope I'm not barging in. I left a message saying I'd like to stop by."

Slowly, she started to put the words together to explain what had happened.

"I've just been over to the property I told you about. Where I was supposed to meet the trust officer, Garret. Well, when I walked in, the place was a mess and it was full of hate literature. Pamphlets and stuff for the Caucasian Nations." She didn't feel ready to add that Garret himself was nowhere to be found.

"No lie?"

"This thing has taken a whole different turn." She pulled off her boat boots and then started tossing paper and kindling into the woodstove to distract herself and release some of the tension she was feeling.

"Ruthie, I've never seen you so stressed."

Ruthie felt like saying that Fioretti hadn't seen her be a lot of things, and that she hadn't invited him anyway. But she knew it was the worry talking, and she held her tongue. Besides, she didn't feel entirely safe being alone in the cabin.

"Is that your message light blinking?" he asked, and she turned away from the stove to look. She hadn't even noticed.

She pressed "play" on the machine, hoping it was a message from Garret or something more from Diane. But it was a new message from Fioretti, saying he was getting close to the cabin. He gave her a small smile as they stood there listening to the recording. If she hadn't been so worried about Garret, the whole thing might have been awkward. As it was, she was mostly cold and tired. She called her boss and left a voice mail, telling him she'd been to the police in Concrete. She called Garret's bank and talked with someone on the switchboard, trying to remember his boss' name.

Fioretti managed to get the fire started. She stood over the stove rubbing her hands together, and told him about Arnie and about Gibbs' racial comment to Garret and how he sabotaged the donation.

"I'm sorry, Ruthie. This Gibbs character sounds like a disaster."

"I just have no clue about what to do. If he was waving a weapon around, well, then anything's possible. I hate to even think about it." In her mind's eye, she could see Gibbs forcing Garret out into the woods somewhere. She warmed her hands, realizing her clothes were still damp. The McGowan property was big enough for Gibbs to be hiding out on, and forcing Garret and Diane in hiding with him. "I should have gone back there, to the property, with the sheriff. I shouldn't have wimped out." She started to get choked up.

Fioretti patted her on the back. "Ruthie, don't blame yourself. If this guy is that much of a wacko, you shouldn't be walking into—into a crime scene. You did the right thing, getting the cops in there. They're probably doing a search in the woods." He stood next to the stove and looked her in the eye. "You're one of the strongest people I know. And one of the smartest. We've got to figure out our next step."

"*Our* next step?" She almost smiled then. Maybe it wasn't such a bad thing he'd showed up. If Garret called for her to come and pick him up somewhere, Fioretti might be able to supply some kind of reinforcement like be ready to get the police. "Fioretti, you don't have to get dragged into this."

"Look, sweetheart, I don't know what you think of me after all these years. But right now, it doesn't really matter. Right now, you're in a bind. And old Fioretti is going to do everything possible to help you out, even if it's just moral support. If this trust officer, Garret, called for help, wouldn't he call here first?"

She nodded. "I sure hope so."

"Then you need to be here for now. I think you should stay here until you hear something more from him or the police. Let's fix you some hot tea and then we'll figure out what to do next. If we need to do some investigating on our own, well, better done in twos, mia cara."

Diane was coughing into her gag. Garret heard Gibbs mumble something about not wanting to waste gas by turning on the heat, but when he spoke it was mostly just to mock his wife, telling her he liked her better with her mouth shut.

Garret felt exhausted, spent from the tension of the hours trying to hold off Gibbs and from being driven around cold and blindfolded lying on top of piles of boxes, but he couldn't let himself drop his guard. He started thinking of song lyrics to try and stay focused. Carmen McRae singing Monk came to him.

You're takin' off weight, well you needn't, you're lookin' just great, well, you needn't... You're actin' sincere, well, you needn't, you're callin' me dear, well you needn't, It's over now, it's over noooow...

Having been away from the music for a few years, he was becoming more aware of what jazz had done for him when he'd let it. When Garret had stayed in practice on his horn, jazz had been about listening and describing what was happening in the moment. It gave you that edge, kept you in the present, because your mind stayed right there. If you let your mind wander, you had to drop out. You'd have nothin' to say that would fit. Jazz was the quintessential opposite of spewing out some notes from a line of sheet music; it trained you to be alert, to read the signs around you, to prepare for anything. If you really paid attention—following its surprises, noticing what was being left out, listening for the players to comment back and forth on tangents, referencing the bigger question all the while—it could teach you as much when you listened as when you played.

It taught the very type of instincts and intuition that might have kept him out of his current bind, in fact. But he had let it go. He'd let it go when he needed it the most.

He realized Diane had stopped coughing and wondered if she had fallen asleep. If she'd really called the cops and left a message on Ruthie's voice mail, someone could be looking for them now. If she'd lied, there was almost no chance that anyone would know something was up. But if Diane was in on it, what purpose did he serve?

After what seemed like over an hour of level highway with some stop-and-go traffic, Gibbs and Abbot started arguing about which way to turn again. Gibbs mentioned something about Coeur d'Alene.

So that was it, Garret thought. Roy had mentioned that the Caucasian Nations had their compound at a place called Hayden Lake which was near Coeur d'Alene, a town east of Spokane just across the border into north Idaho. But why bring a black dude to the compound? Could they have thought they could use him to front off the cops? Crazy as it sounded, that might be it, Garret thought, as he tried to shift his weight off his side again. Maybe they were going to stick him in the front seat when they got closer.

After a long stretch, they turned right, and Garret's body slid a few inches to the left. The boxes below him started clanking again as the van continued down a rougher stretch of road that felt like unpaved gravel.

"All right, Abbot," he heard Gibbs say suddenly. "Here's your turn. Go down this road about a mile and we're home free."

The van swung right again, and the engine seemed to rev in a lower gear. Garret heard Abbot bragging about how this was "a place where men could be men and brothers could be brothers." Garret was sure they were heading into the compound.

"This is the real God's country," Gibbs was saying. "Now, they're expecting us, right?"

"Course, they just don't know what time. Because like I said, I had to stop usin' my phone. We're a little early, is all." The men were silent for a minute. "That's two of their security guards up ahead, looks like."

The truck came to a stop and Garret heard Abbot roll down the window.

"Hi there," Abbot said to someone outside. "Say, I've got a delivery for Scott Jamison."

"Oh, is that right," a man's voice said from outside. Garret didn't think it sounded much like a question. "Hold on a minute." The guy talked into a radio that was putting out a lot of static. "What kind of delivery?" the voice outside asked.

"Oh, Mr. Jamison knows all about it. Regular supplies, you know. Food. Mostly canned food."

"Oh, from Washington, huh?" The radio buzzed in the background.

"Yes, that's right. Say, are you security with the Nations, or what?"

"I am now, yes." And then after a moment, "Step out please. We're going to need to see your license and registration."

"What's this about?" Abbot persisted. It sounded like Dan was fumbling in the glove compartment.

"Are you going to step out or what?"

There was the distinct rumble of another vehicle pulling up behind them, and Garret held his breath to listen more closely.

Abbot muttered something to Gibbs, Garret heard the words 'gag' and then the door slammed as Abbot climbed out of the van. He heard Gibbs cut Diane's gag and blindfold, reach over and cut Garret's, and then he cut the rope binding their hands and feet together using a large jackknife. Garret squeezed his eyes shut and blinked to get them lubricated.

"Could I just speak to Mr. Jamison?" Abbot said, farther away now.

"That's going to happen shortly," the guy said. They started walking toward the back of the van. "Now, you say you brought food. Where from in Washington, exactly?"

"Well, from Pasco. From Tri-Cities."

"I didn't know there was moss is Pasco. I thought it was pretty dry there." Abbot didn't say anything, and then the other man continued. "So, how come your tires are coated in moss?"

"Oh, well, I was over west of the mountains before I got to Pasco." Abbot was talking too fast. "Look, what's this about?"

"We're going to need to see your cargo, that's what. Now." The guy was getting closer to the back of the truck. "And I'm going to need those keys. Jefferson, this guy doesn't seem to want to play ball. You stand over there, buster. If you must know, this place is under occupation now, and your buddy *Jamison*," his voice reflecting a certain amount of contempt in the name, "is in jail. Along with five people from this compound, including guards and leadership. Any more questions?"

After a moment of silence, Garret heard the man say, "Jefferson, get these two cuffed. That's right."

Suddenly there was a loud grating rumble and bang of metal on metal, and the doors on the back of the van were being pulled open.

There was another loud clang as the other guy opened the side door of the van. "What's going on?" the man closest to Garret said. "Get out of the truck, all of you. Stand over there next to Sergeant McManus."

As he and Diane got out of the van, Garret saw a long narrow driveway with tall thin evergreens on the right and a clearing on the left where a police car was parked. Beyond the long driveway was a large grassy field and two buildings connected by a walkway—one with a sloped roof that looked as if it had a big swastika painted on it. Behind it a tall tower stood two stories above it.

The guy led Garret and Diane away from the van, grabbing Garret firmly by the shoulder, so they were standing next to Gibbs.

"So what have we got here?" the guy, Mack, asked from the back of the van. "Property of Ft. Lewis? Oh, that's cute. Look at this, Jefferson. This truck is full of M-16s and all sorts of army weapons and ammo. Christ. Okay, folks, you're all coming with us."

"Actually, this isn't our stuff," Gibbs insisted, his arms cuffed behind his back. "We just got hired to drive this thing, but we have no idea what's in there."

"Right. And what's your story?" he said, talking to Abbot. Abbot just shifted his weight from one foot to the other and kept quiet, his eyes on the ground.

"Officer, these guys have been holding us hostage," Diane said. Her voice sounded hoarse.

"That's right," Garret said. "They shoved us in that van and tied our hands and feet and blindfolded us."

"Sure thing. I've heard that one before, too. You got nothing to do with this, right? Wrong place, wrong time?" He took a step towards Diane. "You're all coming with us, see? No questions."

"What about our vehicle?" Abbot asked.

"What about it? You're transporting military weapons across state lines and who knows what else." He looked hard at Garret for a minute. "You were all passengers, so as it stands right now, you're all accomplices as far as we can tell. Anyway it's not up to us. Any story you've got you need to explain down at the station."

"It's not our stuff," Abbot said weakly, finally finding his voice. "We're just a delivery vehicle."

"Tell that to the judge."

Ruthie tried calling Rhea McGowan again but there was no answer and no machine.

"Ruthie, you've been on the phone all this time. How are you going to know if anyone is trying to call?" Fioretti asked. He was right. The cabin's old land line would just ring busy. "I don't think it's going to help for you to sit here in wet clothes and stew about all this. You've got the police working on it. Why don't you get into some dry clothes, and I'll fix you something to drink."

She showed him where the white wine was that she had bought the day before. It was supposed to be for her and Garret.

"Would you like me to make you some supper? I could run into town and get some groceries," he offered.

"It's okay. I've got plenty here and most of it's already fixed. I think you're right. What I really need to do is warm up." Now that she was off the phone, she realized she still felt chilled.

She took a hot shower, and started to feel better as she pulled on her fleece pants and sweater. Fioretti was right—there was nothing she could do now but wait. Wait to hear from Garret, wait for the police to do their jobs, wait for her boss to apply some pressure. She needed to stay calm.

The halibut had been marinating in the small fridge next to the wine, and she pulled it out onto the counter. It was supposed to be for her dinner with Garret, too, but she was going to have to stop being maudlin about it. Putting the halibut under the broiler was easy, and while it cooked she fixed a tossed salad to serve with the pasta salad. The small dining table already had two places set and for a moment, looking at it, she started to feel worried again.

Fioretti noticed her studying the table. "All set? What can I do?" Ruthie shook her head and started putting the food on the table. As if remembering something suddenly, Fioretti held up a finger and went out to his car. When he came back in he was carrying a small loaf of French bread and cheese.

He poured her a glass of wine and gestured for her to sit down and relax, almost as if he were directing a play or a movie. She felt like an actor taking orders, hollow, wired from adrenaline but exhausted underneath.

"Ruthie, I truly hope this thing comes out okay. Here's a toast to cosmic intervention—that the life of your friend is safe." He lifted his glass, and held it for a moment before adding, "And the lives of *all* those you hold dear, and that I hold dear." He took one sip. "And among those whom I hold dear, you are at the very top."

His sudden earnestness surprised her, pulled her out of her thoughts. "Thank you, Fioretti. I don't know what to say."

"You see, that's why I am glad to be here with you now. I know you're troubled, and there isn't too much I can do to make you feel better, but... " his voice trailed off as he took another sip and looked at her, apparently at a loss for words.

"It's okay," she said, taking a small sip from her glass. The entire day was starting to feel surreal. "You're helping a lot. I've never dealt with anything like this before."

She just picked at her food, though the fish was tasty. She'd marinated it in lemon juice and Italian herbs to impress Garret.

"This is spectacular," he told her. "Really delicious. That's one thing I don't do much of—cook something out of the ordinary. But I enjoy eating good food."

"I remember." How could she forget? Even in high school, Fioretti had always posed as the connoisseur of good food.

He poured her some more wine even though her glass was still nearly full.

"I'm having trouble containing myself, so—," he set the bottle down between them. "I'm sorry, Ruthie. Sorry for being selfish. My life has been pretty intense over the last decade. I've been fortunate, I guess—doing the projects I want. But…" He paused and glanced down at the wine bottle which he began to turn absentmindedly, then suddenly he stopped. He shook his head and looked up at her with that intense gaze of his. "I may have reached a plateau. I'm not sure where I'm going anymore. And then here you are, and I think... You're fantastic. Here's a woman who's so bright and natural and talented." Fioretti looked down as though he had run out of things to say. For once he seemed to have no verbal reservoir to tap into.

"Fioretti, there's nothing wrong with your style, okay? I'm glad you haven't lost your—your artifice, so to speak."

"Well, that's encouraging, but I've never thought of you as being aloof."

At first she wasn't sure what he meant by that, though she wasn't meeting him half way emotionally.

"I've spent too much time cultivating sarcasm," he continued. "But not you. You were the one with heart." He waited, but he was still talking about the past and she thought they had already covered that ground. When she didn't comment, he seemed to choose his next words carefully. "I was devastated that night after the Wild Ginger when you left my parents' house all of a sudden. Were my fantasies jumping ahead of the so-called real world? I was trying to come up with a rational explanation... for why you left."

"It seems life is never simple."

"I was afraid you'd say that. I hoped it was just that you didn't want to be in my parents' house, but I knew it must be something else. Someone else, most likely... It's this other guy, isn't it? This... Garret?"

She nodded. It *was* Garret.

There was no more denying it, especially not to herself. The urgency she'd felt, that foghorn in the dark warning her to leave had been like a message telling her that Fioretti would never be really right for her. She'd grown up. And without meaning to, she'd developed feelings for Garret which made her underlying feelings of dread all the more intense. She thought of his hand around her waist and his gentle smile as he'd taken her for a little turn on the dance floor. That feeling had followed her; it had been building the entire week. Doing the needed chores to get the cabin ready for his visit—cleaning, buying the right food, splitting wood—had built up a pleasant sense of anticipation within her that was almost sensual.

"But, Ruthie—what's wrong with me? Is it because I can't dance?" Fioretti was keeping it light, perhaps to protect his ego.

Ruthie had to laugh. "Don't be absurd. And anyway, you just think you can't dance."

"Then, what is it? What is it about this guy?"

"I don't know, Fioretti. Things just happen. You know that better than anyone. Remember how you used to rave about avant-garde film directors, about people who insisted on improvisation? You used to agree with them, that feelings mattered more than some complicated script or philosophy, that real life was more like looking in a kaleidoscope. Constantly shifting. To your credit, Fioretti, you've still got it, and I don't think you'll ever settle for anything less. Why should you?" She lifted her glass then, as if the gesture could accentuate the argument.

"But for me, emotions are harder to deal with than work. Harder, even, than art," he said.

"Well, sure. They're always new and unpredictable, and we rarely have words for them. I'm just trying to let the feelings through. But Fioretti, it's going to happen to you—emotional attachment you can't control."

"Merda." He stood up suddenly, and started looking through her CD case.

"What's wrong?"

"Well, it already has, is all."

She watched him for a moment and then headed into the kitchen. She wasn't about to probe into that one.

Chapter Ten

†

"Look, Warden, these guys were holding me hostage. I had nothing to do with their hair-brained scheme to sell those weapons. I got dragged into this." Garret was hoarse from repeating himself. "When am I going to get to use the phone?"

"In a few minutes, soon as the sheriff gets back. We're short-handed around here. Thanks to you and your buddies around the corner, we're full up." The overweight warden, gray at the temples, re-hooked the large key ring onto his belt.

"Don't listen to him, Warden." Gibbs was in the cell next to Garret's. "He acts confused and innocent, but he's with us."

"You're wasting your breath on me, both you guys. You'll have to tell your problems to the FBI," he said, looking distracted.

The warden had another set of keys on a big metal ring that he held in the crook of his elbow. He re-checked both their cell doors, shaking them hard.

Garret added, "This is such a complete hoax. My lawyer is going to clear this all up."

Gibbs forced a laugh. "Yeah, right. I s'pose you keep some guy on retainer, just in case you decide to sell a few stolen army guns."

"The bank backs me in work situations, even for something as wacko as this." As Garret said it, he started to wonder how far they'd go. "I'm sure of it."

"Don't count on it. Those big corporations, they don't give didley squat about your ass. Once you show 'em you're a little out of the ordinary, they decide you're expendable—they'll find an excuse to transfer you upstairs to some dead end job. Next thing you know, you're out the door. No, I've got a guy who can really handle this thing, show those guns weren't ours. Period. It's just a matter of time."

The warden paced back and forth with his thick squeaky shoes, his keys jingling with each step. "You don't get it, Gibbs," he said smugly. "Nobody in Kootenai County is going to set any bail for you guys, see. This is an FBI thing now—FBI and ATF. They're calling the shots. You might as well get comfortable. Both of you." He stopped in front of Gibbs's cell and glared inside. "And you can stop yelling to Abbot. He's out of earshot. In fact, he's out of anybody's earshot. As far as that goes, we haven't even seen bail set for Briggs, Jamison and the rest of the CN, and they're on county charges."

"What the hell did they do, exactly?" Gibbs asked.

"Not that it's your business," the warden said as he started to pace again. "Two of their security guards shot at a woman and her son who were just driving by. She stopped her car on the side of the road, 'cause her son dropped his wallet out the car window, and then her engine backfired."

"So they thought somebody shot at 'em?"

"That's what they say. But they assaulted this woman and her son. Luckily, they're still alive. Plus Briggs and Jamison, they say they've never heard of you, or Abbot, or any of ya'll."

Gibbs exhaled loudly, and the warden stopped in front of his cell again. "It's guys like you who made us keep this thing quiet. We're a small understaffed county, see, but we're not just staring at our navels. We saved the feds a big hassle by getting these guys behind bars before things got out of hand. It's guys like you who are ruining the state of Idaho." The warden shook Gibbs' cell door again and then left.

"Well, that figures. You didn't really expect the Caucasian Nations to recognize you publicly, did you?" Garret started to cough.

"Hell, they're already in deep shit. My story is, I was delivering some boxes with a buddy and we didn't know what was in 'em. We were just hired to drive the vehicle, like one of those drive-away companies. It's better that they don't recognize us. The cargo belonged to the owner of the vehicle. Period. In fact, since you were in back, I'm gonna tell 'em you were the liaison to the cargo, far as I knew."

"Make up all the crap you want, but there's no evidence I was in on it. I'm just a bank employee and my boss'll vouch for that. She knew this situation was volatile. Plus Abbot's not going to come up with the same story. That's why they're keeping you separated. You're in deep shit, deeper than the Caucasian Nations. That's what's pathetic—you're fighting their battle for 'em, and now you're the one with federal charges."

"So you got it all figured out, is that it? Your class in criminal law's really paying off for you now, is it?"

"You can keep up all your snide bullshit, I don't care. Seems to be your specialty, anyway, scapegoating whoever's handy. Just like you did with Diane." As far as Garret knew, Diane was in the women's section of the jail.

"What the hell do you think you know about her?"

"Hard to say. She's a tough one to read. But the way you kept putting her down at the cabin was blatant misogyny. Even with you acting like a total jerk, she wasn't dumping on you every chance she got. It ain't that different from how these hate groups try to scapegoat Blacks and Jews. I feel sorry for you, Gibbs. I really do. You idolize this group but you don't really know what they're up to."

Ruthie stacked the dishes in the sink and went back into the small living room, trying to think of who else she should call. At least her boss was working on it but she didn't know if he had reached Garret's boss yet. Fioretti was playing an Erik Satie CD—a very Fioretti-like selection—and was writing in a notebook.

She moved the rocking chair closer to the wood stove and sat down, warming her feet close to the sizzling embers, rocking back and forth slowly. The heat warmed her muscles, making her feel elastic. All this waiting and tension and worry left a metallic taste in her mouth.

Suddenly the phone rang, startling her, and she realized the sheer power of the wood heat had almost caused her to doze off. She jumped up from the chair and grabbed the receiver of the old wall phone after the third ring.

"Hello?"

"Ruthie, it's me. Garret."

"Oh thank God! I'm so glad you called! Are you all right?"

"I am now."

Garret's voice was low and tired, and Ruthie stepped into the kitchen to hear him better over the music.

"Look Ruthie," Garret continued, "I'm in jail over in Coeur d'Alene. I got captured by Gibbs out at the McGowan place, and then he got arrested for transporting stolen weapons. I was in the van, so right now they've got me as an accomplice." He explained that the Caucasian Nations leaders had been busted shortly before they arrived. "I called the bank on their 800 number to try and get this lawyer I know on my case, but I need you to call my boss Sybil at home, and ask her to help me out. You can get her under directory assistance in Seattle. Sybil Bancroft."

"Of course." Ruthie grabbed a piece of paper and a pen from the counter and scribbled down the name. "Garret, I want to come over there. I can get there quick, and maybe it'll help."

"Sure, it might. Come if you can, sugar. It's the county jail in Coeur d'Alene. They say it's by the fairgrounds." Ruthie heard him take a deep breath. "You stay cool, Ruthie. It's all gonna work out."

After she hung up, Fioretti came in the kitchen and she explained it all to him in a rush of relief.

"I'm going to fly to Spokane if I can get something right away," she said excitedly. "Alaska's got flights all day long."

"I'm coming with you."

She gave him a quizzical look. "Why?"

"Ruthie, what you've got going here is history in the making. You may not see it yet, 'cause you're in the middle of it, but what you and your friend are witnessing might be the beginning of the downfall of the Caucasian Nations."

Ruthie wasn't thinking about the bigger picture right now. "Maybe so, but I just hope my friend doesn't get dragged down in the process. Thank God he's okay! I never thought I'd be so glad to hear somebody's in jail." She did a tap dance on the kitchen floor.

Garret tried to get some rest in his cell, even though there was racket coming from all directions and the lights overhead were intense white fluorescents that glared through his eyelids. He covered his eyes with his jacket and pulled an itchy woolen blanket from the cot over his body. The slamming of cell doors seemed to vibrate the entire jail, but he didn't really mind. Being liberated from the rags stinging his wrists and chafing against his mouth was relief enough for now, and being allowed to piss and to drink water felt like a luxury.

In the cell next to him, Gibbs was breathing hard. Garret thought he sounded like he was asleep, though that seemed unlikely. With the bright lights, the reverberation of doors slamming, the loud voices, and the warden pacing back and forth jingling those keys of his, Garret couldn't imagine anyone sleeping. As if in explanation, he heard Gibbs ask the warden for a decongestant on his next pass.

"So what's your scam now, Gibbs?"

"It's no scam. I get allergies sometimes."

"Oh yeah? Sometimes, eh? I'll see what we got."

"So Carter, you still awake?" Garret shifted the jacket over his eyes and made a small sound as a reply. "Good. So, you're so perceptive, do you think Diane will ever be able to forgive me?"

Garret gave a small harsh laugh of disbelief. "What do you mean, 'could she forgive you'? You sold her down the river, Gibbs. Just like you're trying to do to me. You *kidnapped* us, remember?"

"I was protecting her."

"Do you honestly think she'll buy that? Protecting her from who? You manipulated her dad's will. You held her at gunpoint. You brought in another thug, who also held her at gunpoint and tied her up 'cause you said so."

Garret heard Gibbs get up and take a piss and then clear his throat. "Look, it could have turned out a whole lot different."

"You mean, like if you managed to score on that sale and make a bunch of money? You said yourself you were just going to split when the deal was done. So don't pretend you were working towards some fairy tale ending, Gibbs. You'd be up to your ears in multiple counts, regardless."

"I'm going to try and get her extricated from it, since she had nothing to do with it."

"Yeah, that'll just make everything better," Garret said. "What a nice guy." Who did Gibbs think he was, anyway?

"Look, the two of you showing up at the cabin threw a curveball into our plan. No one was supposed to be there. I just—I overreacted and it got out of control."

"You can't just claim some temporary lapse in judgment when you've done the things you did today, Gibbs. She won't buy it and I don't. This wasn't some fluke, it took planning. It took time."

"Okay. But the plan involved me and Abbot. So I got caught up in his scheme, got swept away by it. But the plan never involved Diane. I'd like to tell her that she wasn't ever supposed to know. She wasn't supposed to get hurt."

"Oh, how honorable. You hear yourself right now? What you did was off the charts. Period."

"It was just a mercenary deal with the Nations. I wasn't planning on joining up."

"Course you're gonna say that now. Man, I can't believe this." Gibbs was pissing him off all over again. One minute he's talkin' white pride, and now he's losing sleep over what his wife thinks about him. This guy was seriously wack. "Course you're gonna try and save face, take advantage of the fact they won't recognize you publicly. But you sounded damn sympathetic to their cause back there in the cabin. I bet if they hadn't been busted, you'd be chanting their slogans right now, sitting in some hall counting your dirty money, learning their rituals. As far as Diane's concerned... What? You thought maybe she'd come around to their cause?"

"I don't know. I didn't have that worked out yet."

"Let alone what you had in mind for me."

"Look, once the deal was done, we would have released you. Let you out over in Spokane or someplace."

"Sure you would have," Garret said, bunching his jacket behind his head like a pillow. This guy was too much. "Just let me go? Like you didn't think I'd report you?"

"The CN used to have a certain sovereignty, like an Indian tribe almost. They were protected. They used to be able to keep the cops out of there, more or less. I thought I'd be alright."

"In your dreams. You run your mouth too much to ever be alright. Don't think I forgot that comment you made." The fluorescent glare was giving him a headache. He could hear the warden's keys jingling down the hall.

"Hell, you act like a goddamn detective." Gibbs sighed.

"It ain't that. I'm just a curious person, though obviously not curious enough this time. Black people are born being more aware; it's just about survival. I should have blown the whistle on your smug ass from the beginning. You gave me enough clues, man. I get an F for this whole fiasco." Garret tried shifting his weight to relieve his back pain. "First, I could have gotten blown away in the process, and second, I wasted almost two months screwing around with your bullshit. I'll probably be on probation at work now, if I even keep my job. My job's about closing philanthropy deals, not enabling anti-social pathological syndromes. I'm trying to find clients who want to improve society. But you wouldn't understand that, you—"

Gibbs cut him off, and Garret hadn't realized how loud he'd gotten. His throat was sore. "Okay, okay. You wear me out."

"Whatever that's supposed to mean," Garret said, rubbing his eyes.

"I never met anybody like you."

"You mean you never talked to any black dudes about anything serious before."

"It's not that. It's just, seems like your values are connected to your work."

"Well, I put more emphasis on actions than theories. You and this Caucasian Nations thing? It's pathetic. They put all this emphasis on race. Black and white. But people don't choose their race. And race isn't a matter of black and white or red or brown these days, anyway. People choose their actions, not their race. You don't think about what it is you're *doing* Gibbs, not really. That's why I don't get you."

Gibbs was quiet for a few minutes though Garret could hear him pacing slowly. Finally, he said, "You could have blown me away in that cabin after you got the gun away from me. You would have gotten away with it, too. Self-defense." He heard Gibbs blow his nose.

"What are you gettin' at, Gibbs?"

"See, if I had been in your shoes, I'm pretty sure I woulda gotten so pissed I'd have lost it and pulled the trigger. Prob'ly would have blown everybody away."

"Like a lot of people, you've got a short fuse."

"So, it got me thinking. You handled that pretty well, getting control of my gun. Then Abbot shows up and you drop your weapon, you know when to fold 'em. So you have a keen survival instinct, good reflexes, and you know how to stay calm in a tense situation."

"Maybe I still got that at least."

"And… you're a goddamn lawyer! You've got this whole idealistic thing going with your job. This society thing. In a crazy sort of way, what you've got is like a luxury."

"Integrity, you mean?" Garret asked. "You think it's some luxury?"

"That's what I mean. You have integrity."

"Well it ain't a dirty word, Gibbs, and you don't got to act so surprised. It can feel pretty good, too, though sometimes it's hard to figure out what the integrity move is in a particular situation. Like right now—I could be resentful as hell, 'cause here we are talking about you and your predicament. Why should I care? Why is it the black dude always gotta be helpin' somebody, always gotta be stepping in to deal with the next guy's problems? You got me in this shit hole, and I'm mad as hell and sick to my stomach. I got a thing for this girl and who the hell knows where she's at really and I'm laid up in here."

"You got a thing for that conservation chick?"

"Right. So-called. Ruthie, the botanist and dancer. But I don't know where I'm at with her, and I haven't heard a peep out of the bank or any lawyer either. Let alone how things might get twisted and how I might be associated with this hate group. Sounds pretty crazy to me. But, then I think, maybe, just maybe you're saying you might want to re-think this whole Caucasian Nations program. Seems like that might be what you're gettin' at, and if it is, crazy as it seems I gotta go for it. You see what I'm sayin'? I gotta go for that, 'cause in this particular point in time, that's the integrity move. Hopin' that somebody like you is going to have a turnaround. Even if the chances are only one in a million. You know why?"

Gibbs didn't answer.

"'Cause quiet as it's kept, it's an unspoken rule for a hell of a lot of black people in this country that if somebody is talking about becoming more human, we got to stop the presses and opt in."

"Okay..." Gibb's blew his nose again.

"Course that's maybe more about me than about you. Part of my DNA that I barely know about. I'm no psychologist but I had a girlfriend once who was. She believed people could change. She worked on that all the time, like her life depended on it. And you know, I think it did."

"What happened to her?"

"She dumped me. She fell for some other guy. Some guy with bucks, actually."

"You don't seem all fucked up about it."

"It took me awhile, but no, I'm not. Not anymore. I had to forgive myself is what happened."

"Well, I never totally flipped out, okay? I just lost my sense of direction falling for Abbot's scheme. I never had anybody really believe in me, see. Not my parents, not Diane, not anybody."

"Look Gibbs. I don't know your story and if I did, I'm not sure I'd understand it. All I can say about that is there's nobody makes a man but himself." Garret's father used to say that and now he understood what he meant.

The more Garret tried to relax his muscles, the more he felt soreness in different places. He couldn't tell if Gibbs was putting him on or not. His shoulders, his lower back, his arms and legs were all sore. The hours of tension now adding up to pain. So Gibbs might be practicing for what he might say to the judge. Or practicing what he might tell his lawyer if he got one. Garret was too exhausted to read this guy. When he closed his eyes, all he could see were the faces in the cabin. Gibbs staring him down. Diane slowly retreating into a muted robot. The stillness, the tension. The cell doors slamming in other parts of the jail seemed like branches hitting the roof of the cabin. And Abbot. How close had his bullets come? If Garret had been standing, it'd be all over now.

Garret heard the warden's squeaky shoes and keys jingling. Suddenly, Gibbs hollered out of the cell door.

"Say warden, this guy Carter? He wasn't with us. He's just a banker who got dragged into this thing by mistake. I was putting this deal together, so I had to bring him along, but he had nothing to do with it."

The warden stopped in front of Gibbs's cell and shook his head. Garret leaned closer to the bars so he could watch.

"You know, Gibbs, you might as well save your breath. Like I said before, you're all going before a judge on federal weapons charges, and there's no way around that. As for you being a credible witness, I ain't holding my breath on that one either." He shook the bars and walked a few feet away.

"Thanks, warden. I knew I could count on you."

Garret took off his shoes and tried again to get comfortable. "Say, warden," he hollered through the bars. "Any chance you could dim the lights a little?"

"Oh, we already did that. Can't you tell?"

"Dang," Garret mumbled, and pulled his jacket back over his eyes.

In his dream, Garret was at the airport on the walk-way outside of baggage claim waiting for Sybil to pick him up for his job interview. The airport was busy, and he watched each new vehicle appear, unloading luggage, picking up passengers, navigating around all the transport vans and buses mixed in with the noise of planes taking off. When he finally called her office to see what was taking so long, Sybil picked up the phone. "You thought I was serious about that job interview?" She cackled, and her laughter got louder and louder until she finally hung up.

It started to rain. He had no raincoat. Garret watched the buses, vans, and taxis come and go, knowing his job in Chicago was long gone. He had nowhere to go. He had no return ticket, no apartment. He was exhausted, and all he could think to do was grab a cab, try and rest up in a cheap hotel for a couple days, and then move to the Y.

A cab pulled up and he recognized the driver. It was Gibbs. As Garret got in the back seat, Gibbs said, "I'm off duty now, but since I recognized you, I decided to stop." The inside of the cab was warm and damp. The wipers were going but the windows were all fogged up. Garret realized there was a woman in the front seat looking into a compact mirror. Gibbs glanced back at Garret briefly and adjusted the rear view mirror. "Carter, this is my ah—date. Ruth Adams."

The woman glanced back at Garret and nodded briefly. "Pleased to meet you."

"But…" Garret didn't understand. Why didn't Ruthie recognize him? How could she have forgotten? Her window was open slightly and fog and mist penetrated the car from outside, surrounding her. Garret thought maybe the fog was making her forget, like a cloud of amnesia. If only he could remind her of the dance class, but he couldn't find the words. His mouth felt gagged.

Gibbs laughed and turned up the radio. Garret thought maybe he imagined the dance class, maybe even the whole thing with Ruthie. Now he would have to get over her, just like he'd done with Jackie. "Well, then, can you recommend a cheap motel that's not too far from here?" he asked Gibbs.

"Hey, the cheapest thing's right here at the airport. Forty-nine bucks at the Jet Motel. Course you'll hear the planes all night. Long as you got a good set of earplugs!" Gibbs laughed again but with abandon this time, and pulled out into traffic.

"All right, Carter. Your lawyer got your charges reduced to county charges, and now the D.A. has dropped the charges altogether." The warden unlocked the cell noisily, pulling Garret out of his light uneasy sleep. "You're outta here."

"No shit? What time is it?"

"Uh, it's about 3:00 a.m."

Garret realized it wasn't the same warden. It was a different guy with the same sets of keys, the same pair of squeaky shoes.

"There's some girl out there saying she won't leave until you get out." He pulled the door open.

"Some girl?" Garret was still thinking of his dream, remembering the total lack of recognition on Ruthie's face and Gibbs's loud mocking laughter.

"Says her name is Ruth Adams."

"Music to my ears." Garret was up then, tucking in his shirt.

"She got the police station in Mt. Vernon calling here, and got your lawyer on the job. They had some answering machine tape, saying that Gibbs here was brandishing a weapon."

"What'd I tell ya?" Gibbs sounded wide awake. "Congratulations, Carter."

Garret put on his shoes and the warden led him out of his cell.

"Look Carter, I'm sorry about what I did."

"Okay, sure. And from the looks of things you're going to have lots of time to think about it. But it doesn't matter what I think. Your life is yours, man. In here or out there. La vida. La dolce vida. I learned something from you anyhow. That you can never go to sleep. Never. It's about eternal vigilance. So I won't be hangin' back like I was. I won't be the one who's just goin' along to get along. I won't go around trying to be twice as good. So there was something in this for me after all."

Garret got his wallet back from the officer who handed him release papers to sign and washed up. When he got to the lobby, there she was, waiting on a hard wooden bench.

She rushed over to him and threw her arms around him and gave him a kiss. Any doubts he'd had were gone now.

"Oh Garret! What a relief!"

"God, you been waiting a long time I bet." He took a good look at her face, and then realized she wasn't alone. He looked over at the guy standing behind her.

"Garret, this is Cameron Fioretti, an old friend from high school. He came over with me to help me take care of things."

"Garret—I hope you're okay," Fioretti said as they shook hands. "I just came along for the ride, really. Say, I got us some rooms over at the hotel in Coeur d'Alene."

Garret got the feeling that something had transpired between Fioretti and Ruthie, but he let it go. It had been too long a day. "Thanks, man," he said to Fioretti.

They watched as Ruthie went over to the bench to pick up her backpack. "You know," Fioretti said in a confiding tone, "she's had a fire under her the whole time, working to get you out of here. The lawyer tried to put her off until tomorrow, but she wasn't having it."

"I don't doubt it. She's about the strongest woman I've ever met."

"I know. Strong and persistent!" Fioretti gave him a thumbs up.

Garret sensed a hint of ambivalence, so shielded that he'd be hard pressed to call it envy. And even if it was, this guy seemed too sophisticated to let it show, as if his rough edges had been filed down by a sculptor.

When he got to his room it was almost four in the morning. As he emptied his pockets, somebody knocked on the door.

"Room service!" announced a voice from the hallway. A guy brought in a big tray of fruit, bread and cheese and champagne.

"Yikes! I didn't know this was coming. Well, here ..." he said to the attendant, handing him a few bucks.

He called Ruthie in her room and asked her about the order. "Sounds like Fioretti is up to his old tricks again," she said. "He probably thought you'd be hungry."

"Well, at least come and help me eat this!"

When Ruthie got there he was uncorking the bottle. "Apparently this friend of yours doesn't do anything halfway," Garret said.

"No, not Fioretti."

"Plus, he's probably crazy about you," Garret gave her a look out of the corner of his eye, "and wants to make sure you're going to be okay."

"There may have been a time he felt that way," Ruthie said, smiling shyly at Garret. "But, well..."

"He may think he still has some kinda chance?"

"I made it clear how I feel. I stopped worrying about him a long time ago." She smiled at Garret. "This looks pretty good."

She put some food on two plates and Garret poured the champagne.

"Okay, Ruthie. Here's to you, for helping me get out of jail tonight, for being such a beautiful soul, for being an activist and never giving in, for being a great dancer and … well, for being just plain beautiful!"

She laughed heartily. "And here's to you, for keeping it together the last twenty-four hours, for being smart and savvy, and for staying positive!" She started to lift her glass and then added, giggling, "Oh, and you can dance!"

They took a few sips, and then he gently kissed her warm sweet mouth.

Chapter 11

†

In his dream, Garret was back in jail. The warden told him he would have to go to trial, that he was accused of the same thing as Gibbs, and that he had no attorney, unless the public defender could squeeze him into his schedule.

He heard an alarm—a fire alarm, maybe. Or maybe the other inmates were starting a breakout. He could go for that.

Suddenly, he was awake. As the dream faded, he recognized the hotel room and Ruthie next to him, the long thick gold curtains, and the table next to his side of the bed. He looked at the clock to see it was almost 11:00 and realized the phone was ringing.

"Hello?"

"Is this Garret Carter?" a man asked on the other end of the line.

"Yes. Who's this?"

"This is Daryl Lacey. I spoke with your colleague Sybil Bancroft who gave me this number. I've been retained by Mrs. Rhea McGowan to look at these purchase and sale agreements related to some property up on the Skagit River. Do you have a minute?"

"Oh, sure."

"Mrs. McGowan said that she would like to proceed with this transaction, to donate land to the conservation group in exchange for a charitable gift annuity."

"Well now, this is good news."

"And she said that she would like to apologize for the behavior of her son-in-law."

"Let's just put that on the back burner for now," Garret said, noticing that Ruthie was awake now. She pushed her hair out of her face and pulled the sheet up around her, smiling curiously.

"Thank you for being so understanding. I do have one further question. Our appraisal came out to $1.1 million, which appears to be slightly over what you had discussed?"

"That's right." He smiled at her and gestured "yes" with his thumb up.

"All right. On the timber cruise section of the appraisal, it says that the fish and wildlife department found a bird called the Marbled Murrelet, which is now listed under the Endangered Species Act. They've concluded that under these circumstances, the highest and best use for this property is conservation. Mrs. McGowan has already signed off on it. She signed the $1,000,000 contract you gave her, and we're considering the other $100,000 as a donation. Does that sound alright with you?"

"Fabulous. By the way, Mr. Lacey, did she say why she wanted to proceed with this?"

"She said her CPA called it a win-win situation, and it was what her husband wanted to do."

"I would agree on both counts."

"I'll courier the signed agreements over to you on Monday." They hung up.

"Ruthie, you're not going to believe this! This dude, Rhea McGowan's lawyer, said she signed the papers! The appraiser said the highest and best use for the property is conservation!"

Around noon at the hotel brunch, Garret and Ruthie filled their plates with melons, crêpes, biscuits, and turkey sausages from the elaborate buffet.

"All this food around suddenly makes me feel like I was in a prisoner of war camp," he said.

"*Mm-hmm,*" she said, adding fruit to her plate.

She'd convinced him to go for the big brunch, saying that the place was famous for it, though he would have been satisfied with another mouthful of her voluptuous curves. They had taken the back stairs down from their room; she skipped down them like a girl getting ready for a hopscotch contest, and he felt as if he could have floated.

Fioretti was at a table overlooking the lake, sitting across from an attractive forty-ish looking woman. He was asking a waitress for coffee refills as they sat down, and as she walked away he introduced them to Kathleen Parker-Steel. "A journalist from Spokane," he explained.

"I recognize you!" Ruthie said. "I recognize your name from the Spokane paper!"

"Well, thank you. I sometimes wonder if Seattle people ever read our paper."

"Say, Fioretti, thanks for the scrumptious midnight snack," Garret said, settling in at the table. "Or should I say early morning snack. You really shouldn't have."

"Yes, I should have." Fioretti smiled and the waitress brought more coffee cups.

"And this is one hell of a view of this lake. It looks huge," Garret added.

"It is huge," Kathleen said. "About three miles wide here and twenty-five miles long." The lake was surrounded by forests and gentle hills and mountains in the distance dusted with light snow.

"And we're up more than 2,000 feet above sea level here," Ruthie added. "You know, Kathleen's been on the case over here in Spokane, sometimes the lone voice of reason as far as Hanford downwinders are concerned."

"Which is why I invited her to join me for brunch today," Fioretti said.

"God, Fioretti, you really don't waste any time, do you?" Garret added.

"I hope not."

"Cameron tells me you've just been through an ordeal—brushing up against the Caucasian Nations," Kathleen said, looking at Garret.

"Well that's right."

"We're finally getting the sheriff's office to go on record about these latest arrests. But Cameron and I think there may be a larger story here."

"Maybe material for a documentary," Fioretti added. "I was reading that the Rand Corporation called the Caucasian Nations the first truly nationwide terrorist network in the U.S."

"That's right," Kathleen said. "This group has been claiming they want to make the Northwest a haven for people like them. Well, I don't think so!"

"We want to interview the Native American woman and her son who were chased and shot at and finally beaten," Fioretti added. "It's a gruesome story. And we're going over to the jail to see if the CN leadership—if Briggs and his boys will talk.

Fioretti was writing in a spiral notebook. "Garret, I'll want to talk with you after some of these interviews, to help me sort some things out. Okay with you?"

"Works for me." Garret spooned strawberry jelly over his crêpes.

"What about this guy Gibbs? Would you say he's more of a mercenary or a real sympathizer with the C.N.?" Kathleen asked.

"Honestly, that's hard to say. In jail he claimed he wanted to rethink his position with the C.N. though he might just be rehearsing for his court date or his lawyer—if he gets one."

"Well now that the leaders are in jail, some of these sympathizers may crawl back into the woodwork," Kathleen said. "I read about a skinhead who was a leader of one of these hate groups back east. He had a turnaround when he realized his kids were growing up with so much hate, they'd end up in jail. He went public with this and now he's a spokesman for a human rights organization."

"Isn't this close to where they made that movie 'Smoke Signals'?" Fioretti asked.

"Sure. The Coeur d'Alene reservation isn't far. That's one of my favorite movies, as a matter of fact," Kathleen said.

"Oh, I loved that movie," Ruthie said. "It felt so real. That singing in the beginning when that house was burning—it gives me chills just thinking about it."

"I gotta see that," Garret said.

"It's a story of place and forgiveness, and the enormously purging quality of the Spokane Falls at the end," Kathleen said.

"Maybe we could fold the Spokane Falls into our documentary as a sort of homage," Fioretti offered.

"And the landscapes around here with these high elevation lakes," Kathleen said. "People don't realize how beautiful it is. And most of the locals … they don't sympathize with the CN. No way."

"I'm just brainstorming, but it might be powerful to suggest that people can purge themselves of mistakes or errors in judgment. Even within the expansion of these groups like the Caucasian Nations," Fioretti added.

The waitress came back and filled their coffee cups again. Garret thought Fioretti had to be on some kind of roll.

"So Fioretti, it sounds like you're planning to stay around here awhile?" Garret asked.

"As long as Kathleen and I can get this thing moving, this is where I need to be. As for getting you two to the airport, you give me the high sign whenever you're ready."

“I’d like to get back to Seattle pretty soon. Ruthie and I have been working on a deal that seems to be on the verge of getting done. Sealing this deal and hopefully saving my job, as long as the next deal doesn’t involve paying quite as many dues as this one.” Garret rolled his eyes.

Fioretti laughed and then gave Garret a high five.

“And… you’ve got a gig coming up early in the week,” Ruthie reminded him.

“Well, yeah. It’s really just an open mike thing with Vance. This woman knows my life better than I do,” Garret said, looking at Fioretti. He could have kissed her then, but he didn’t want to rub it in.

“I can’t wait to hear you play!” Ruthie added.

Later that afternoon, Fioretti drove them to the Spokane airport. As they headed to the entrance, Garret asked about the impressive cliff-like columns of rock rising up out of the arid landscape in the distance. Ruthie told him they were columns of basalt, porous and lava-like. Rays of sun cast a rose-colored glow over patches of snow in the foothills in the distance.

Fioretti parked and walked them to the gate. When Ruthie went to the restroom, he said to Garret, “The biggest screw up of my life was letting her get away when I did.”

“We all make mistakes, man.” What could he say? He knew it was easy to screw up. He’d done it himself.

“I figure, with a girl like her, you really only have one shot.”

“You may be right.” Garret was still euphoric from the night before, in no mood to be analytical.

“I’m interested in this story, but the real reason I came out here with her was because I wanted to make sure it was for real between you two.”

“I know,” Garret answered, though he wasn’t about to gloat. Not with somebody who was trying to keep his ego in check.

"When I saw you two this morning, there was no doubt in my mind," he added.

"No doubt in mine, either," Garret said. "Especially after the way she handled things while I was in jail. She's the reason I got out when I did—with your help, of course. Thanks for pitching in. And good luck with your documentary project. It sounds like it could be super important."

The glass doors were being opened and passengers who had lined up at the bottom of the steps started filing out to the small prop plane that would take them to Seattle.

Ruthie reappeared from the bathroom and picked up her bag. "Thank you, Fioretti. Thank you for everything you've done."

"I wanted to." He smiled at her. "I couldn't do much, but I wouldn't have missed it for anything."

"You've acted like a real friend from start to finish, and I appreciate it." She gave Fioretti a hug.

Through the open doors, Garret could hear the propellers begin to turn slowly, a mild sputtering whir, then speed up, chopping time, punctuating their words and drowning some of them out.

Garret noticed Fioretti pause as if he had some final words for Ruthie, but he seemed to be tongue-tied, and the propeller got louder and faster. In that moment, watching Fioretti search for the right thing to say, he recognized in him a man with not only a mission, but also a burden. For a second, it sent a chill through Garret, reminding him of his conversation with Gibbs as he was leaving the jail. He'd promised himself he wouldn't be one of those people who just goes along to get along. Garret had pledged to try and do the right thing, no matter what. He knew that more than anything else, this was why Ruthie was getting on the plane with him.

Garret shook Fioretti's hand, meeting the same firm grip he'd felt the first time they'd met. "Stay in touch, man. Let me know how I can help with your CN project. And I'm not just sayin' that." Fioretti looked him in the eye and nodded, saying he would.

After take off, Ruthie dozed against his shoulder, reminding him they had slept some in the morning, a sleep that had been so deep for him because he finally knew she was right there and he didn't have to worry anymore. They would take turns carrying the weight, the two of them. He'd never felt like this before, letting someone else share the weight. But he'd been alone with his burden long enough. He didn't know the extent of what she carried, but whatever it was, he was willing. He was stronger now.

In a few days he'd be at Tula's, hook up with Vance and do a set. No doubt they'd play some of their regular tunes, but he thought now he had some others, too, and the colors of these few days would penetrate through the chord changes—the rain forests, the rivers, the mountains, the arid lands, like the cliffs of porous basalt with their splashes of color, and the flow of the ancient floods carving out the earth's coulees and gorges creating creeks, streams and rivers all the way to the ocean, to the tides of infinite time, the tunes, the phrases would speak of constant movement, constant change—and the big difference now, more than any other feeling meandering through the faces of the ones who mattered, now the feeling would be gratitude.

NOTES

†

Chapter 3:

The Seattle newspaper, *Real Change*, was created in 1994 to address issues related to poverty and homelessness. In 2013, 16,000 – 22,000 papers were sold each week. Nearly half of the vendors were homeless.

Chapter 5:

During a speech at the University of Washington, Dr. Cornel West stated that philanthropy is no substitute for social justice.

Chapter 11:

Following the arrest of two Aryan Nations security guards and leaders, the Southern Poverty Law Center brought a civil lawsuit Keenan vs. Aryan Nations on behalf of Victoria Keenan and her son who were assaulted by Aryan Nations security guards when Victoria Keenan stopped her car in front of the Aryan Nations compound to look for her son's wallet.

In September, 2000, a jury issued a judgment of $6.3 million against the Aryan Nations. The founder of the Aryan Nations relinquished his 20-acre compound to the Keenans in a bankruptcy auction. The Keenans sold the property to a philanthropist who later donated it to the North Idaho College Foundation.

In 1996, Time Magazine interviewed T.J. Leyden as a former skinhead. From 1996 – 2008, Leyden worked for the Simon Wiesenthal Center. In 2008, his book "Skinhead Confessions: From Hate to Hope" was published.